BP

"We've Never Been Married!"

It had not been marriage as she understood the word.

"Don't talk nonsense," he said impatiently, shifting uneasily. He had always avoided discussions of this sort. He wanted to be free to fly away whenever he chose without feeling that he had left any problems behind him.

"We went through a legal ceremony," she threw back. "But as far as a real marriage was concerned, you never even considered it. You put a ring on my finger, took me to bed, and then went back to what you really enjoy—your job. You've never taken me seriously."

"You're wrong." He moved nearer, a harsh light in his eyes. "I take you very seriously."

LAURA HARDY

is one of Silhouette's top-selling authors. She and her husband of many years live with their children off the northwest coast of England on Britain's lovely Isle of Man.

Dear Reader:

Silhouette Romances is an exciting new publishing venture. We will be presenting the very finest writers of contemporary romantic fiction as well as outstanding new talent in this field. It is our hope that our stories, our heroes and our heroines will give you, the reader, all you want from romantic fiction.

Also, *you* play an important part in our future plans for Silhouette Romances. We welcome any suggestions or comments on our books and I invite you to write to us at the address below.

So, enjoy this book and all the wonderful romances from Silhouette. They're for *you!*

Karen Solem
Editor-in-Chief
Silhouette Books
P. O. Box 769
New York, N.Y. 10019

LAURA HARDY

Burning Memories

Silhouette Romance
Published by Silhouette Books New York
America's Publisher of Contemporary Romance

Other Silhouette Books by Laura Hardy

Playing with Fire
Dream Master
Tears and Red Roses
Dark Fantasy

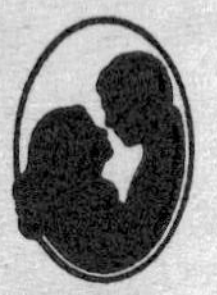

SILHOUETTE BOOKS, a Division of Simon & Schuster, Inc.
1230 Avenue of the Americas, New York, N.Y. 10020

Distributed by Pocket Books

ISBN: 0-671-47447-2

First Silhouette printing May, 1981

10 9 8 7 6 5 4

America's Publisher of Contemporary Romance

Printed in the U.S.A.

Burning Memories

Chapter One

London was asleep, but the fuzzy glow of the orange streetlights lit the sky for miles. From a distance, thought Nicola, they looked like the campfires of some enormous army. Martin hadn't spoken for some time. They were both tired. They should have left the party earlier, but they had been enjoying themselves and somehow the time had flashed by.

The spring night was clear and chilly, the stars bright pinpoints of light. As they reached the top of Highgate Hill, London lay stretched below them, a cluttered huddle of roofs, spires, tower blocks, with a sickle moon climbing the sky behind them. Nicola stared sleepily at the city, snuggling into her warm, thick wool jacket.

"It was a good party."

Martin started, glancing sideways at her. "Wasn't

it?" Broad and fair, he had a comforting solidity about him and he never said much. Nicola did not mind that. She didn't talk much either. Martin was frowning, though, which was unusual. His calm good temper was one of the qualities which had drawn her to him.

"Have you got something on your mind?" she asked him. He had been very cheerful all evening. Whatever was bothering him had only come up during the drive.

"You," he said, smiling.

"Me?" She laughed. "That's nice. Why, especially?"

He took one hand off the wheel and touched her knee caressingly. Nicola stiffened. She knew Martin sensed that involuntary withdrawal but she couldn't help it. Her cheeks glowed with anxious color.

Martin did not wait for her to say anything. He took his hand away, grimacing. "You see?" he asked. "That's what is on my mind."

"Oh," Nicola said, fighting down a desire to shift away in her seat.

"We're neither of us children," Martin pointed out. "We've been seeing each other for months now but we never seem to get any further than a good-night kiss."

"I can't; not yet," she stammered, her fingers twisting in her lap.

"Look, I respect your point of view," Martin came back quickly, his face coaxing. "I do understand how you feel, Nicola, but can't you understand how *I* feel? You can't say I've tried to rush you. I've been patience itself."

She sighed. "Yes, you have. I'm sorry. I can't . . ." She broke off and Martin looked at her sharply, the streetlights giving him a clear view of the tension in her trembling mouth and worried eyes.

It was not the first time they had had this discussion. With some men, of course, they would have started to argue on the subject after a first date. Martin had been less impatient. He had realized, perhaps, from the start that it would do him no good to try to rush her into bed, but, in any case, Martin was not the type of man who rushed anything, especially in personal relations. He was cautious, methodical, his own valuation of himself too high for him to want to grab at an instant pleasure. Martin took himself seriously.

The car drew up outside her home and he turned toward her, his eyes half apologetic. "Don't look so upset," he said, smiling wryly. "I shouldn't have brought it up tonight. We're both tired. But your attitude is old-fashioned, Nicky. People aren't going to condemn you, you know, even if they found out. Hasn't anybody told you? This is the age of sexual freedom. You do your own thing." He used the phrase with a rueful grimace and Nicola laughed.

"Maybe my own thing is to wait and see."

He put a hand to her cheek, his fingers caressing. "You are exceptional, do you know that? I meant what I said. I admire your integrity. It may mean I have to wait too, but you're well worth waiting for."

Her doubtful little smile made him laugh. He bent forward to kiss her with lingering tenderness, his fingers still stroking her cheek. "Am I still invited to lunch tomorrow?"

"Of course," she said, getting out of the car. "I was planning on roast chicken."

"Great," he said. "I'll bring a bottle of white wine. See you at twelve?"

"Twelve," she agreed and stood watching his red taillights streak away into the darkness before she let herself into her flat. It was on the ground floor of a large Victorian house. Nicola had been living there for over two years. She had spent time and energy on making it a comfortable, pleasant home. Standing in the living room she looked around her, shivering slightly. It wasn't just the cold dead of night which sent that tremor down her spine. She felt, as she always felt when she came back here, abruptly alone, as though suddenly aware of a pressing silence, an emptiness. Martin's company, hours spent with friends in lively talk, could chase away that loneliness for a while, but the moment she walked back into the flat it all fell back on her like an icy wave.

With a sigh she walked into the bathroom, inspecting her face as she removed the traces of makeup. Her skin was very pale, the translucent pallor emphasized by the frame of black hair curving around her face. Her eyes had the golden warmth of some amber liquid, their dark pupils lending depth to them, but that warmth disguised the obstinacy which lay behind her gentle smile.

She always had a rapid shower before she went to bed. Stepping under the warm water she closed her eyes, feeling the relaxing spray jet down her back. Why had Martin brought up the subject of sex? It had been the last thing on her mind. She wanted to go to bed tonight only to sleep. She did not want to carry any worries into the bedroom with her.

A white toweling robe hung by the shower. Yawning, Nicola wrapped it around herself and switched off the bathroom light. The shower had done its work, leaving her warm, relaxed and increasingly sleepy. She walked into the bedroom, put a hand to the light switch and then shrugged. The darkness was inviting and so was her bed. She wouldn't bother to put on the light and look for a nightdress.

Walking across the room in the dark she took off her robe and dropped it on the end of the bed. Turning back the thick, comfy quilt she slid underneath it, her body turning onto its side, searching for warmth.

A split second later she was wide awake. Her body had touched another body.

With lightning speed her nerve ends flashed their message to her brain. There was a man in her bed.

She screamed. At the same instant she leaped out of the bed, grabbing her robe and huddling into it with shaking hands as she ran. Her cries of panic were involuntary but her mind was working as she screamed. The phone was in the living room. Could she get there before the man caught up with her? He was moving, she heard the bedsprings creak. Would anyone hear her? And would they come if they did? People in a big city tend to ignore strange noises in the night. They don't want to get involved. They might ring the police but by the time a patrol car got here it might be too late.

"What the hell are you doing?"

The voice stopped her in her tracks. The bedside lamp came on and she turned, her face incredulous.

The man in the bed was staring at her, his bare brown shoulders gleaming smoothly, rippling with muscle as he ran one hand through jet black hair, brushing it back from his face. A sardonic smile twisted his mouth as Nicola stiffened, speechless and slowly flushing.

"What are *you* doing here? How did you get in?" She did not recognize her own voice. It sounded dry and rusty, as though she hadn't used it for a long time.

"I used a key," he drawled.

"A key!" She repeated the word helplessly, trying to think, her mind in total disorder. She did not like the way he was looking her over, his blue eyes oddly bright and mocking. Fumbling with her belt she tied the robe more tightly under those bright, watchful eyes.

"Forgotten I had one?" His mouth twisted again, wry humor in his face. "So had I, to be frank. Lucky I remembered it."

"What are you doing here?" she asked again, recovering from her first shock. "I thought you were in Africa."

"I flew back today."

Something in the way he said that made her look at him sharply, her gaze flicking over him in search of some visible sign of injury. That was usually what brought him back to London. Had he been caught in crossfire again?

He registered that hurried inspection and laughed shortly. "No, I'm not hurt."

Nicola reacted with a flare of angry color. For a moment she had experienced the old familiar fear, the anxiety, the pain, and she was angry now. "Get dressed and get out of my flat," she ordered tartly.

"Don't be ridiculous—at this hour?"

"The hour has nothing to do with it. This is my flat and you have no right in it."

"As I recall, I paid for it," he pointed out drily. "That gives me some rights, I think."

Nicola's teeth came together with a grinding hiss. "Get dressed and go!"

She felt at a distinct disadvantage standing there, her slender body so inadequately dressed in that thin white toweling robe, her legs bare to the thigh, her damp hair ruffled after the shower she had had before she came to bed. She would have liked to pretend she was unaware of the constant lazy inspection of those blue eyes, but she couldn't quite convince herself.

He gave her a shrugging grin. "I'm not going anywhere."

"You are," Nicola insisted, meeting his gaze with determination. He regarded her, his eyes narrowed now, then he slid over and switched off the light. In the sudden darkness he said, "To hell with you. I'm going back to sleep."

Nicola's temper boiled over. She marched across the room and switched the light back on, looking with rage at the tumbled black hair against the pillow. "Who do you think you are? What do you think you're doing? Walking into my flat . . ."

"Our flat," he interrupted.

"My flat; mine," Nicola seethed.

She was so angry that she missed the wicked look in his blue eyes. "Our flat; ours," he said and Nicola began to tremble with fury.

"I'm not going to argue with you."

"Oh, good," he said and she caught the bland note and gave him another angry glare.

"This flat is mine. We agreed."

"I don't recall agreeing."

"Your solicitor did!"

"Did he, indeed? He didn't have my consent to that."

"Whether he did or did not, that's not the point."

"I'd say it was very much the point," he murmured, eyeing her with amusement.

"I'm not getting into one of your endless debates about definitions," shrieked Nicola. He would never concede a point. He had nearly driven her out of her mind with his infuriating circular habits of arguing.

"Why are you shouting?" He sounded so calm and reasonable and he was nothing of the kind. Nicola looked at him with dislike.

"Get dressed, give me back the key to my flat and get out of here."

"Can we discuss this in the morning?" He yawned again, sitting up, the quilt dropping off and giving her a clear view of his bare wide shoulders and his deep chest, the tanned skin roughened by wiry dark hair which curled up from the flat planes of his stomach.

Hurriedly averting her eyes, Nicola said, "No, we can't discuss it in the morning. I want you out of here tonight."

"Nicky, I'm dead on my feet," he said plaintively.

"I'm tired too," Nicola retorted. "But if you think I am allowing you to sleep in my bed, you're wrong. In fact, I'm not even talking to you while you're in there, so you can get out of it now. We'll discuss this in the living room."

She should have realized she had made a mistake in making that statement. He gave a mock sigh, his wicked blue eyes fixed on her. "Oh, well, if you insist . . ."

Her pulses leaped with alarm as he pulled back the quilt, his bare legs sliding out. Turning, she fled into the other room while he laughed behind her. Over her shoulder she told him, "Get some clothes on before you come in here."

"My word, you're a shrew," he drawled.

Nicola switched on the light and went over to turn on the electric log fire, shivering. It was a crisp, cold night. Her robe was too thin and she was tired. This was the wrong end of the day for having a row. Nicola hated having rows; they made her feel ill. She had had too many of them in the past. She had thought all that was over. How dare he waltz in here and take up a comfortable spot in her bed?

She heard a movement and tensed. "Are you dressed?"

"Yes," he said tersely, adding, "although why you should start being coy about seeing me without my clothes on, heaven alone knows."

Nicola turned round slowly, not quite trusting him. He was wearing a short quilted black satin robe. She had bought it for him two years ago. He had hardly worn it, and it looked brand new. She skimmed a glance over him reluctantly. She had never quite got used to the vital impact of his appearance. He was a tall, lean man, with a physical magnetism which kept you staring at him, especially when he moved; his body in motion had a powerful grace, the muscled elegance of some predatory creature. That impression of lethal force was echoed in his face, his features strong and sardonic, his blue eyes electric, their intelligence masked by mocking humor which was visible in the lines of his mouth too, the hardness sometimes curving into aware sensuality when he smiled.

It was a long time since Nicola had been able to look at him. A pulse began beating in her throat as she looked hurriedly away.

"Is this going to be a long session?" he asked drily. "Because if it is, I could do with some whiskey. It's bloody cold in here."

"It isn't going to be a long session." Nicola meant it to be short and far from sweet.

He put his head to one side, surveying her with wry comprehension. "I wish I could believe that, but you have that obstinate look again."

"It would save us both time and trouble if you would just get some clothes on and go."

"No doubt," he agreed. "But it *is* the middle of the night and I'm exhausted. What do you expect me to do? Camp out in the middle of Trafalgar Square?"

"I don't care what you do. You're not staying here."

He pushed his hands down into the pockets of the

robe, his wide shoulders grimly set. "I can see I'm going to need that whiskey."

"There isn't any," Nicola retorted.

"No whiskey? I must say, your hospitality has taken a downward turn since we last met," he said, walking over to the cabinet in which she kept drinks.

"Do make yourself at home, won't you?" she told the back of his black head with frustrated fury, watching him as he took out a bottle of red wine which she had been saving for some evening when Martin came to dinner.

"Is this all you've got?"

"Yes," she flung at him. "Sorry."

"How about coffee?"

"Look, I want to know what you are doing in my flat!"

Ignoring that, he padded off into the kitchen, his bare feet silent on the cream-colored carpet. Nicola looked around the room, biting her lower lip. Maddening, she thought. He is every bit as maddening as he ever was—what am I going to do?

She followed him out to the kitchen and found him hunting through the contents of the refrigerator. "Cream?" he asked over his shoulder and she said through tight lips, "No."

"You know I like cream in my coffee," he complained.

She counted to ten. If she hadn't, she would have screamed. "Since I was not expecting you, you can't be surprised if I haven't got any cream."

He found a jar of powdered cream substitute. "This any good?"

"I like it," Nicola said. "If I didn't, I wouldn't have it."

"That's what I like about you," he said. "Logical." The mocking little smile got absolutely no response.

"Stop trying to put off our discussion."

"Was I?" He made the coffee, stirred in the powder, and bent to sniff at the result with apparent enjoyment. "Ah, coffee, the smell of real instant coffee. The stuff I've been drinking smelled of ground acorns."

"Steve!"

He swung around, the electric blue flash of his eyes making her throat close in alarm. "So, you *do* remember my name."

Her flush mounted and her stare became even angrier. "I don't think that's funny."

"I wasn't being funny," he told her, and let his eyes wander down over her from her damp hair to her bare feet. "That's just how I used to imagine you." He paused. "Well, almost," he added wickedly. "Minus the robe."

Her face made him laugh under his breath. "Stop looking as though I'd broken in here with intentions on your virtue—all I want is a few hours sleep."

"Why didn't you go to a hotel?"

His face altered, the amusement vanishing and a strange grayness creeping up over his skin. "I was tired," he said tersely. "I wanted to sleep. I haven't slept for three nights."

"You can sleep in a hotel."

His mouth twisted. "I can't." For a moment he stared at the coffee. She saw the fixed brooding tension in his whole body. "I had to come here," he added.

Nicola watched him, frowning. Something was seriously wrong, she suddenly realized. There was some indefinable difference in him. He looked fit enough—the long body had the same poised vitality, the potential menace of a cobra in it. Under his smooth bronzed skin, however, he was taut, strung-up, on edge. She could believe him when he said he hadn't slept for three nights. His blue eyes had a deepset, burning exhaustion in them. His mouth had a drawn look. A tiny muscle jumped at the corner of his eye, indicating some nervous tension.

"What's wrong?"

Her quiet voice disturbed his brooding. He looked around, thrusting one sinewy hand through his thick hair. "I've had a bad week," he said lightly. "One of the worst weeks of my life." Picking up one of the mugs of coffee, he handed it to her and she automatically accepted it, her trembling hands clasping it tightly, the warmth of the hot liquid seeping into her palms.

Walking past her with the other mug he sat down next to the log fire, holding one hand toward it. "I'd forgotten how cold London can be at this time of year."

"We're having a slow spring," she agreed, sitting down on a chair opposite.

He sipped his coffee, his heavy lids half closed. "How's the new job?"

"I like it." She had been working in the features department of the paper for six months, since just after Steve had left that last time. She was used to the job by now. It was a much slower way of life and reassuringly calm. She wouldn't go back to the way things had been before.

She hadn't been taking much notice of the news since her change of job. After several years in the newsroom she had been glad to forget the daily adrenalin rush of the news. It filtered through, of course, via the television, and her occasional glance at a newspaper, and she knew there was a civil war going on in the African state where Steve had been working. That was what had taken him out there, after all. Steve only turned up in trouble spots. War and the rumor of war brought him zooming in like a carrion crow.

She looked at him, torn between cynical anger and a reluctant anxiety. What was wrong? She knew that shuttered face. Steve never talked about his job. He wrote his stories and what you got from the curt paragraphs was all Steve ever betrayed.

His reputation had been based on the cool, rational reporting of what he saw. Steve was not the sort of reporter who used adjectives to excess. He was objective; he just told the facts. He was famous for his terse, crisp style and the unblinking eye which saw so clearly.

"The paper knows you're back?"

"Of course. They were expecting me today."

"I'm glad somebody was," Nicola said, brushing back a few loose strands of black hair from her cheek.

"I thought I'd surprise you," he drawled, looking amused.

"Oh, you did that, all right."

He laughed, the blue eyes sparkling. "Scared you stiff, did I?"

"What do you think?" She was furious, remembering her terror as she had leaped out of the bed and run for the door. "I had no suspicion it was you. I haven't seen anyone from the newsroom for weeks."

His lip curled sardonically. "No regrets?"

There was far more to that question than a simple inquiry about her views on changing her job, but she pretended not to understand that. "None," she said coolly. "I don't miss the newsroom. Life is much easier in features."

"Dead boring, you mean." He swallowed some of his coffee, his bare throat rippling. His tan was so deep it seemed to be imprinted on his skin, increasing the dangerous brilliance of those blue eyes. He had always had a tan of one sort or another; he took the sun easily.

"Can we cut the polite conversation? We still haven't got anywhere on the subject of what gave you the idea you could walk into my flat—and my bed—without so much as a polite request."

"You weren't here to ask. The flat was empty."

"Why didn't you ring me at work?"

"I only flew in at nine o'clock tonight." He threw her a sarcastic grin. "If I had asked, what would you have said?"

"No way," she admitted, meeting his eyes.

"That's what I thought." He finished his coffee. "If the discussion is over . . .?" He rose, the movement displacing his satin dressing gown and giving her a brief, disturbing glimpse of his hair-roughened thigh.

Looking away hurriedly, she said sharply, "It isn't. You don't seem to get my point. You had no business coming here. You don't live here anymore. I do. So get dressed, get out and give me back my key."

He put down his mug with a crash which made her jump. "Look," he snarled, "I'm going back to bed. Any further argument can be postponed until the morning. I'm going to sleep and I don't want to have any early calls, either. I'll wake up in my own good time."

As he walked away she went after him, trembling with anger. Nicola had always thought of herself as good-tempered. It had taken Steve Howard to teach her that she could be so angry that her head could feel like it might blow off. She grabbed at his arm, her fingers digging into the quilted satin, and he halted to look down at her.

"Haven't you forgotten something?" she demanded. Was he going to ignore the fact that they were getting divorced?

He eyed her, his mouth crooked, a weary quizzical mockery in the lift of his brows. "Yes," he said slowly, then his hands were fixed on her slender shoulders and before she could evade him he jerked her against him.

"You dare," she burst out.

His mouth had already fastened onto her lips as the words left them. Parted, trembling, her mouth had no hope of escaping his abrupt, sensual possession.

She grasped his arms to push him away but there was an ache somewhere deep inside her, a burning sweetness pouring through her veins, and while she hesitated, Steve kissed her deeply, one hand sliding down her back, pressing her toward him so that she felt the tense masculinity of his body from breast to thigh.

Shuddering, she broke free, a shaking hand at her lips. "That's enough!"

"It will have to be, for tonight," he said huskily, giving her a slight grin. "I'm too tired even for you. I'm so tired I can hardly keep my eyes open."

He had gone before she had a chance to stop him. The bedroom light went out; she heard the bedsprings creak as he turned over heavily, giving a smothered yawn.

This is insanity, Nicola thought. I can't let him do this to me. He has no business walking into my life again. He is selfish, thoughtless, ruthless. Her hands clenched at her sides, she stood there trembling with anger, staring at the open door.

Marching over to it she stared into the room. The light from the room behind her fell in a pale shaft across the carpet, showing her the dark head buried in the pillows.

Nicola slammed the door viciously.

"Bitch," he murmured in a sleepy voice which held a muffled amusement.

"You're leaving tomorrow morning, the minute you're out of that bed," she yelled back.

He didn't answer. All she heard was the slowing sound of his breathing, a rustle as he shifted under the quilt.

She curled up beside the log fire, staring at the artificial flames with unblinking anxiety. It had been a disaster from the first day, their marriage. If she hadn't been so crazy about him, she would have realized what madness it was to consider marriage with a man who never stayed in one place for long, needed to duel with death as though it gave some desired consummation, was deaf to all pleas for him to change his way of life.

They had been temperamentally unsuited. Nicola was gentle, quiet, domesticated, a girl who never took risks and was terrified of violence. Steve Howard should never have entered her orbit. Working in the newsroom, though, she had met him with the casual collision of fate, an accidental encounter which, if they had known anything about each other at the time, would have had no consequence. All they had known, however, was what they saw. Nicola had been dazed by his electrifying sexuality. Those blue eyes had flashed over her and she had been head over heels in love at first glance.

She was never sure what Steve had seen but he had seemed as instantly fixed by her. Perhaps it was because they were such opposites, both physically and mentally. Nicola was slight and delicate, the warmth of those brown eyes matching her gentle smile, and Steve was not the first male member of the staff to have noticed the seductive nature of her femininity. Nicola was as strongly female as Steve

Howard was strongly male. The polarity of their natures pulled them together from that first meeting.

After their marriage, Nicola had secretly expected that Steve would settle down, give up his roving existence on the foreign reporting staff and take a desk job in London. The paper had offered him several. He was highly thought of—he could have walked into a good job whenever he chose to do so. He refused. Nicola had to learn to live with fear as her daily companion. While Steve was abroad, she struggled to come to terms with his way of life, but her nerves cracked under the strain.

He was so rarely at home and while he was away she waited with terror to hear that he had been injured, or even killed. Her temperament just could not take that permanent, nervous life on a tightrope. Steve's idea of marriage did not match hers. She wanted her husband with her, not on the other side of the world. Steve's electric sexuality and the reactions of other women to it increased their difficulties. Nicola couldn't help wondering what he was up to when he was away for months.

While he was reporting a war in the Middle East he was caught in crossfire and flew home, slightly injured. Nicola gave him an ultimatum. He had to choose, she said. Her—or his job. Steve laughed at her at first, refusing to take her seriously, trying to tease her out of it. Nicola's gentle obstinacy came to the fore. She would not budge. She refused to argue but she kept repeating that ultimatum. "Me—or your job."

When Steve had recovered, he flew back to the

war zone. Nicola at once began divorce proceedings. She got one letter from Steve after that—a terse, sarcastic note which made her so furious that she tore it up and did not reply.

At first she had huddled in their flat, grim with misery. She did not hear from Steve again. Their marriage was over, she told herself. It should never have begun. She began to get angry. She wasn't going to let Steve ruin her life. She forced herself to start going out. At first she went with other girls in the office—theaters, cinemas, parties. At one of those parties she had met Martin. His quiet, dependable kindness had been like a fire on a cold day. Nicola had drifted into seeing him, a little guiltily at first, keeping him very much at a distance.

The quality which had drawn Steve to her was the same quality which attracted Martin. Most men found Nicola's warm gentleness attractive. Nicola had warned him that she was in the process of being divorced. She hadn't been ready to feel emotion again. She was lonely, uncertain, in need of comfort. Martin rushed to offer what he saw she needed. Steve had left scars on her; Martin set about healing them.

He was a patient man. Inch by inch, day by day, he had somehow infiltrated her life. Nicola could not remember actually saying she would marry him after her divorce. The idea had been planted in her mind insidiously. She had become very fond of Martin but she knew she did not feel for him the fierce attraction she had felt toward Steve. That overwhelming passion, though, had led to disaster, and Nicola instinctively turned away from the idea of passion now. Martin's love was so much easier to live with and so much less dangerous. He made her feel loved, cherished, wanted. He made her feel safe.

She did not feel safe tonight. She felt like someone who has gone up to a tiger's cage in the happy expectation of seeing him behind bars only to find the door open and the tiger padding toward her.

Chapter Two

At around three o'clock she got a spare quilt from the airing cupboard in the bathroom and made herself up a bed on the couch. It was four o'clock before she finally fell asleep. She woke up when the newspaper came through the front door, the clack of the letterbox making her wake with a start. Her eyes were dry and ached from lack of sleep. She was stiff, her limbs cramped. The couch was, she had been told when she bought it, designed for conversion to a bed at a touch. A dwarf might have been comfortable on it, Nicola decided, as she got up, stretching. She felt as if she had been on the rack all night.

Going into the small hallway, she brought in the milk and found the newspaper on the mat. She went slowly into the kitchen and got down the percolator. By the time the coffee was hitting the top of the glass dome she had made some fresh orange juice and toast. She sat down at the table and sipped the juice, her weary eyes fixed on the front page of the paper. Her eyes widened and darkened as they read the lead story.

Lowering the paper she looked toward the door. So that was what had put the drawn, haggard look into his face.

A civil war had been raging in the African state from which he had been reporting. It had been a minor affair until now. Steve had become a shocked witness to the acceleration of the struggle. He had seen the wholesale massacre of the rebellious inhabitants of one small township.

How had he got out alive? Nicola wondered, wincing. She pushed the paper away. She could not read any more of it. The details were so painful that even to read them made her feel as if she had been present.

Getting up, she threw her uneaten toast into the bin. Suddenly she wasn't hungry.

Why did he keep on with the job? Hadn't he had enough of seeing death at close quarters yet? One day his luck would run out and he would end up like the men, women and children he had seen mowed down in that African township—shoveled into a hastily dug grave and forgotten about.

She stood looking down at the newspaper, her lips trembling, tears burning behind her eyes.

She snatched it up, crumpled it into a ball and threw it across the room, swearing hoarsely under her breath.

"Temper, temper." The mocking voice made her swing around, tense and feverish, her brown eyes still hot with unshed tears.

Steve ran his glance over her face, his dark brows meeting above his arrogant eyes. "I see you've been catching up with the news." He said that coolly, but his scrutiny was intent.

"You made the front page, don't worry," Nicola muttered with bitter irony.

A harshness invaded his face. "So I should damned well think."

She sagged back against her chair, her body trembling on a low deep sigh. "Yes, it sounds pretty bad."

"You have a genius for understatement." He walked forward, his lean body, clothed only in the black robe, moving with that casual animal grace, and picked up the coffeepot. "This still hot?"

"Yes."

She watched him pour himself a cup, add the top of the milk and sip, his eyes half closed, a tired absorption in his face.

"Was it worse than you made it sound in the story?" she asked, her voice low.

"It was as close to hell as I've ever been."

She drew a painful breath, then her pain became anger and she said icily, "I'm sure you can't wait to get back there."

He shot her a dry smile. "I've been told on good authority that if I try to go back, I'll be shot on sight." That seemed to amuse him. He began to laugh, his blue eyes fierce. "They seemed regretful that they had to let me on the plane at all."

"Why did they?" Nicola was trying to control the helpless shaking of her body, and her voice was only just under the high edge of hysteria.

"I went out with the British Consul. They decided not to risk a scandal."

Nicola was afraid she was going to cry. She had to get away from him before the tears started. She swung around and her chair crashed to the floor. She left it there, and almost ran to the door.

"Going somewhere? What about my breakfast?" Steve inquired in a calm tone.

"Get it yourself. There's plenty of bread and eggs. I'm going to have a shower and get dressed and then I want you out of my flat." She did not wait to see how that was received. The tears were already spilling out from under her lids, trickling down her cheeks. She slammed the door behind her and got to the bathroom before her legs gave out beneath her. Leaning on the door, sobbing and trembling, she felt she hated him.

When the first bitter storm had passed she had a shower, taking her time, the warm water spraying over her skin and easing some of the terrible tension.

She was going to have to get Steve out of the flat before Martin arrived. Martin knew about Steve, of course, although they had never met. All the same, it was not going to be easy to explain his presence in her flat, especially if he was still half-naked. Martin was a good-tempered, level-headed man, but even his calm approach to life might be somewhat strained by the sight of her ex-husband wandering around her flat in nothing but a short robe.

Nicola had only briefly discussed Steve with him.

She had told him as much as she felt he ought to know. Martin had never evinced any real curiosity about her marriage. He had listened without doing anything more than look grave.

"That was no marriage at all, was it?" he had asked her. "He didn't deserve you."

"How true," Nicola had agreed ironically. "I wish he could hear you."

"I wouldn't mind a chance to tell him a few home truths," Martin had agreed. "Men like that have no business getting married at all. He's the type to have a woman in every port. I wouldn't mind betting he doesn't lead a celibate life while he's abroad all those months."

Nicola had ground her teeth. That thought had occurred to her, too. She had sometimes questioned Steve about other women, in the first months. He had been evasive about them.

"No confessions, darling," he had said. "I don't believe in them. After all, what good does it do to rake up the past?"

"So there is a past?" Nicola had demanded, burning with jealousy.

He had turned those electric blue eyes on her, grinning. "Why have your eyes gone green?"

"I've told you everything about my ex-boyfriends," she had said. "Why can't you tell me?"

Rueful amusement had shown in his face. "My past stretches back a lot further than yours, darling. I'm ten years older, remember, and I've traveled further, in every sense of the word."

"I can imagine," she had said tartly.

He had begun to laugh, his black lashes curling

back from his wicked eyes. "Now I'm beginning to feel married," he mocked. "Is this what I'm to expect? You're worse than the secret police. Nicola, there's nothing so dead as an old love affair. Sweep it all under the carpet, all the ash of yesterday. We don't need it." Then he had begun to kiss her, his hard mouth demanding, and, yielding to him, Nicola had let her jealousy slip away.

She pushed away those memories now, too, concentrating her thoughts on Martin. He was always punctual. He would arrive, as he had promised, at midday. So that gave her two hours to get Steve dressed and out of the flat, and before he went she was going to get that key out of him. She wouldn't have him walking in and out of her flat while he was in London.

Dripping, she groped for the towel. It was put into her hands. Her eyes flew open on a reflex action, her wet lashes fluttering back, the brown eyes all pupil in shock.

Steve's blue eyes flashed down over her naked curves and Nicola felt her breasts ache with the inflow of blood under his stare, her body stiffening and fiercely awake. Her breath caught painfully. She wound herself into the towel, hands trembling. "How dare you walk in here? Get out."

"You've lost some weight," he said coolly.

She had lost nearly a stone during the months of their marriage. She had never put it on again. She had always been a very slim girl, but that weight loss had made her waist tiny, her hips even more slender, increased the fragile delicacy of her small face.

"It suits you," Steve decided. "I like girls to be a bit skinny."

She lifted her chin, her eyes defiant, the towel tucked firmly around her breasts and covering her wet body to the knee. Stalking past him she went out, her wet feet leaving footprints on the carpet. This time she not only shut but locked the bedroom door before she dried herself and got dressed.

When she emerged in skin tight blue jeans and a white silk shirt, Steve was listening to the radio in the kitchen. He had had a shower, too, she saw. His hair was curling in damp clusters on his head.

Nicola had decided to try the calm, polite approach. "Now, will you please get dressed and leave?" She stood watching him, her hands on her hips, her freshly brushed hair immaculate.

He switched off the news, glancing at her. "I'm not going anywhere. I'm only home for a week's leave and an in-depth conference with my replacement, then I'm going off to the Middle East. While I'm in London I planned to stay here."

Her head almost exploded. "Are you crazy? Or just plain awkward? You can't stay here."

"Why not?" He surveyed her with a little smile.

She took a long fierce breath. "Steve, we are in the process of being divorced. If anyone found out you were living with me, there could be unfortunate repercussions. You can't stay here. You don't live here anymore."

He yawned, stretching his arms above his head, the movement dislodging his loosely tied belt and giving her an unwanted glimpse of the damp black hair on his chest.

"I'm still tired. I'm going back to bed."

"You dare," she burst out. "Listen to me . . ."

"Later, sweetheart. Right now, I am going to sleep for another twelve hours."

As he walked out, she followed, protesting to deaf ears, ready to throw things if she had to, her fury spending itself without getting any response from him. He dropped his robe without warning, and her nervous eyes flickered over him, from the muscled shoulders and deep chest burned dark brown by the African sun, to the lean hips and hair-roughened thighs. Averting her eyes she swallowed, her skin heated. She knew he was watching her, although he didn't say a word.

He climbed into the bed and stretched, his arms crooking over his head as he yawned. Nicola looked back at him, her hot face irritable.

"Why can't you go to a hotel?"

"Why should I? This is my home."

"Not anymore," she said, on a deep, angry breath. "You're making it very difficult for me." She paused, then said defiantly, "I'm expecting someone here today."

Steve lay still, watching her through suddenly sharp blue eyes, a chill menace in the way his stare fixed her. "Expecting who?"

Nicola was trembling slightly, her nerves prickling with tension. "That's my business. But I don't want you here when he arrives."

"He?" Steve asked very softly, his black brows a heavy line across his forehead.

"Yes," she muttered, lifting her rounded chin to face down the threat in that stare.

"Give him a name." He said that in a terse voice.

"Martin," she said huskily. "Martin Eastwood."

Steve was silent for a moment, then he said coolly, "Well, I'm sorry to louse up your date, of course. I can see it might be inconvenient to have the bed otherwise occupied . . ."

"Oh," Nicola interrupted fiercely, her lips parted on a cry of fury. "How dare you suggest . . ."

He ignored the interruption, his face sardonic. "But my need is greater than his, I'm afraid. You'll just have to make do with the couch."

She was insulted, her body tense. "Martin and I don't . . . haven't . . ." She broke off that stammered denial under his ironic stare, her face scarlet.

"No?" He lifted his brows quizzically. "Poor Martin; what a patient fellow he must be."

"He is," Nicola threw back. "He's prepared to wait until our divorce is through and then . . ."

"He'll make an honest woman of you? Great. Fill me in with all the romantic details later, will you? Right now all I need is sleep, not the secrets of your love life."

He slid down the bed, his eyes closing, and Nicola looked at the bronzed profile, which was all she could see now that he lay on his side, facing away from her. "Look, Steve," she began irritably, and he suddenly sat up, fixing those haggard, glittering eyes on her, the tan not hiding the exhaustion which held his bones in a vise-like tension.

"Damn you to hell," he roared. "Can't you see, you stupid little bitch, that I'm out on my feet? I crawled here because I needed a safe hole to go to—don't you understand? My head's jammed with pictures I don't want to remember, would give the earth to forget. I don't want to talk about the divorce, the flat, your bloody boyfriend. I want to sleep for days on end and forget everything. So get out of here and let me sleep."

Falling back against the pillows, he dragged the quilt over his head, and after a moment of consternation Nicola turned, trembling, to walk out of the room, closing the door very quietly behind her.

She went into the kitchen like an automaton and stood at the window, staring at the sky without seeing it. Steve's rage burned behind her eyelids. What terrible memories had he brought back with him from Africa? It was rare for him to get so involved in what he reported. He had learned, during his years in his profession, to tell the story as he had seen it happen without letting his own emotions get in the way.

She would get no clue from the story in the paper. The subbing staff would have watered down what he had written, carefully softening it for public consumption. Steve, like all the other reporters, constantly complained about that. The paper would never print all of the truth, they said, only a carefully selected part of it.

She closed her eyes, shivering. Why did he have to come here? His long silence had seemed an admission that their marriage was over. She thought he had accepted the idea of divorce. Finding him in her bed last night, all she had felt was anger, but now his outburst had given birth to other feelings. He had made her feel guilty, disturbed, anxious.

It was so unlike Steve to break out like that. He

was a tough, experienced newsman with a cool head and nerves of steel. That, at least, was the impression she, in common with everyone else on the paper, had got of him.

As she surfaced from her thoughts, her eye focused on the low, livid bank of cloud which had spread over the quiet city. A tentative sun was trying to struggle through the gray layers, but the sky was as dull as Nicola's mood. The street was empty. The houses had that deserted look which Sunday usually brings. Most people would be staying in bed, reading the papers, their eyes skimming casually over the horrific news as they drank their Sunday morning tea and hoped the children would not start clamoring for food too soon.

Food, she thought, remembering Martin with a start. He was coming here for lunch and she could not have him here with Steve in the flat.

She went through into the living room and dialed Martin's number. The phone rang for some time. Frowning, she wondered if he was too deeply asleep to hear it, or if he had gone out. After a while she replaced the receiver. She would try again later.

It was difficult for her to concentrate on anything but the man sleeping in her bed. Martin seemed to fade, dissolving like a ghost into the recesses of her mind.

How had she been expecting Steve to react when she told him she was dating another man? Well, whatever she had expected, it had not been what she got. She had not imagined he would make cold jokes about it. Biting her lower lip, she trembled with rage and pain. Did he really believe she would sleep with another man so lightly? Was that the sort of woman he thought she was? The memory of his cynical shrug stabbed her, made her wince.

If that was what he thought, he knew nothing about her, but then, what *did* he know about her? What did she know about him? Their time together had always been so short. Their marriage had been spent largely apart. Had Steve been unfaithful to her? She wouldn't be surprised to find out he had. At the back of her mind she had always suspected it. That had been the most painful of her problems, that suspicion. She had never told Steve that, of course. She hadn't wanted him to know about the bitter fantasies with which she had lived while he was away from her. How could she help suspecting that a man of his sexual vitality was likely to be unfaithful?

Jealousy wasn't one of Steve's hang-ups. If he had really loved her, he would have reacted very differently just now when she told him about Martin. But then, if he had really loved her, he wouldn't have gone shooting off all the time. He would have stayed with her, got a London job, taken her with him if he felt he had to go abroad.

She dragged herself out of her grim thoughts to get the lunch ready. It helped to have something to do. When she had got the chicken into the oven and prepared the vegetables, she rang Martin again, but got no answer. Making herself a cup of coffee she sat down, her brows creased. Where was Martin? Was he on his way here?

A muffled cry made her start, her coffee cup

jerking in her hand. She put it down, listening. The sound came again, louder. Nicola got up and slowly moved toward the bedroom. As she opened the door Steve gave a hoarse yell which made all the hair rise on the back of her neck. He was having a nightmare, his body convulsed under the quilt, his lids flickering rapidly.

She went over to the bed. Steve twisted restlessly, muttering. "For heaven's sake . . ." That came out in a raw agony which Nicola found unbearable.

She could not listen to him. His mumbled words were building up too painful a picture. Sinking onto the bed she caught hold of his shoulders, bending toward him.

"Steve. Steve, wake up." Her voice was shaking and she was very pale.

He jerked convulsively at the touch of her hands, his own hands flying up to clamp over her wrists, their grip like a vise. She was pulled forward, sprawling over the bed. The next moment she was on her back with Steve holding her down, his powerful fingers around her throat. Choking, trembling, Nicola looked up at him in desperation. As she gasped out his name again his lids lifted and she saw the dangerous blue eyes staring down at her.

The locked bones of his face unclenched. His fingers relaxed around her throat although they did not fall away.

"Nicky," he said in a blank voice.

Still trembling, she whispered, "You were having a nightmare."

His mouth twisted. "Yes," he admitted.

"Have you had many of them?" She could guess

the answer to that but she wanted to keep him talking, give him time to recover his balance.

"Yes," he said in a terse voice. There was perspiration on his forehead, beads of it along his upper lip.

A lock of thick black hair had fallen over his temples. Nicola absently put up a hand to brush it back, her fingers lingering on the vital strands, remembering the feel of them, the way the hair had clung to her skin when she ran her fingers through it as Steve kissed her.

"Bad nightmares?" she asked gently.

"Bad enough." He closed his eyes again, shuddering. "Don't ask me, Nicky."

She could not remember Steve ever betraying weakness before. She saw that tiny muscle flickering beside his hard mouth and instinctively put a finger on it to stop it.

He turned his head with a blind, seeking look and his mouth brushed her finger, slid into her palm, the faint tremble of his lips making her heart wince with pain.

"Oh, Nicky, I needed you," he muttered against her skin, the warmth of his breath sinking into her pores, making her blood sing in her ears. "I thought it was my turn any minute. It was so bloody hot. The sun made the place feel like an oven and all around me there was nothing but death. I've never been so angry or so scared in my life. I kept thinking . . ." He broke off, his teeth coming together.

"Thinking what?" she asked, her hand against his cheek, the fleshless angularity of skin and bone alive under her touch.

"When you think you're going to die any second, you can get quite hooked on the idea of being alive," Steve said with grim humor.

She could believe that. She watched him anxiously. Under his tan his skin looked gray.

Had she imagined it, or had he said just now that he had needed her? He had never said anything like that to her before. She had not imagined Steve could ever need anyone. He didn't give the impression of feeling the need for other people which is a part of the human condition. People in general cannot exist alone. They need each other, however briefly, however reluctantly. We are all interdependent. Our lives are knit together in a loose weave and the fabric of one life is never strong enough on its own. Nicola's eyes moved over Steve's face, tracing the strong bone structure which proclaimed his fierce individuality; the arrogant nose, deep-socketed blue eyes, the assertive, self-confident jawline. No, she thought. Steve Howard didn't need anyone but himself.

He watched her and as their eyes met she realized she had been absently smoothing his cheek in the instinctive gesture of comfort one might offer to a child.

Nervously, she pulled her hand away, and Steve smiled at her. "Don't stop, I like it," he said huskily.

"You had better get back to sleep," she said in a low voice. "And no more nightmares."

"Give me something more enjoyable to dream about, then," he murmured in a mocking voice, his hands sliding over her collarbone and fingering the rounded bones of her shoulder sensually, yet the implicit power of those long, sinewy fingers warned that Nicola would not be easily able to unlock their hold on her if she struggled.

"Don't," she muttered, twisting to avoid him but unable to escape those controlling hands.

"What sort of lover is he? The guy you're dating? Sexy, is he? Good looking?" The questions came out drily, a thread of derision running below them, and Nicola hated the way he was talking. He sounded indifferent, amused. He did not sound jealous.

"Martin is a stockbroker," she said and Steve broke into jeering laughter, his blue eyes wicked.

"You're having me on."

Her face irritated, Nicola shook her head and his smile broadened, the lines around his mouth deep in his brown skin. "A stockbroker?" he repeated. "You must have been desperate."

Indignantly she threw back a denial. "Martin is a very charming man."

"Rich, too, I suppose," mocked Steve.

That stung. "I'm not interested in his money."

"What are you interested in? What has he got—apart from this charm?"

"He's attractive. We get on well."

"What do you talk about? The way the market is going? The cost of money? Which company is going bust and who is taking over who?"

Nicola did not like the way he was looking at her or how he was talking to her. His eyes spat blue fire, their mockery cold.

"I'm not discussing Martin with you!"

"I hope you haven't discussed me with him," Steve said, his icy smile going.

"No," she said, her eyes shifting, because of course she had once or twice talked about Steve, although it had been very brief and very cautious.

"Because I would not like that," Steve said through his teeth. "I wouldn't like it at all, Nicola, if I thought you had been discussing me with another man."

"I haven't," she said.

"He does know you're married, though," Steve murmured, watching her closely.

"Of course."

"Then you must have talked about me," he said shrewdly, leaping to the obvious conclusion.

Nicola was annoyed. "Only when I had to—I prefer not to think about you, let alone talk about you."

He did not like that, his brows meeting. "Don't annoy me, Nicola. Take some well-meant advice for once in your life and try not to make me angry. I'm pretty hyper at the moment—if I lose my temper, I could get very nasty."

"Nastier than usual, you mean?" Even as she asked him that she inwardly regretted coming back with that crack. It was a mistake; she saw that as the dark color crept under his tan.

His hands closed around her face, biting into her. "Much nastier," he said thickly just before his head swooped down.

She was angry enough herself to meet his mouth with a furious attempt at escape, her slender body writhing under the pressure of his, bitterly aware of the naked thigh clamped over her own, the wide shoulder pinning her to the bed. She pushed at his chest without managing to shift him. As her palms slid over his warm skin her pulse began to thunder. Her closed lips parted; her open eyes shut. Her fingers dug into Steve's bare shoulders, clinging, holding on with desperate intensity. It was so long since she had been in his arms. Time seemed to rush her away at top speed, back to the first days of their marriage. She stopped thinking and was all feeling. Her hands moved around to the back of his head and clasped it, feeling the vital hair clinging to her palms.

Steve lifted his head to look down at her. Exhausted, limp, Nicola lay with closed eyes, shuddering. She could not meet his stare. She knew what she must look like, her lips burning and parted from those kisses, her skin flushed, her body weak with the desire he had woken in her.

"That's how I remembered you," Steve said huskily.

Slowly her lashes fluttered back. The dazed brown eyes looked up at him, her pupils dilated with passion.

The doorbell rang briskly.

Steve muttered something terse under his breath. Nicola jumped, her nerves wincing at the unexpected noise.

"That," Steve drawled, "is the stockbroker, I presume."

She pulled herself back from the hectic memory of their lovemaking. Defiantly, she said, "I suppose so."

Steve's mouth was crooked with icy humor. "You'd better let him in, then, hadn't you? He sounds like an impatient fellow." The doorbell had rung again, even more briskly. Martin would wonder why she hadn't opened the door.

Sliding off the bed, she stumbled, her legs weak. Steve laughed and she gave him a cold glance.

"What's the matter, darling?" he mocked, satisfaction in the curve of his mouth. "Something bothering you?"

"Nothing is bothering me," Nicola denied. She walked rather less steadily than she would have liked to the door. "While Martin is here I'd be grateful if you would stay out of sight, though," she said as she left, closing the door firmly behind her.

She did not hear any answer but somehow she felt very uneasy as she made her unsteady way to the front door.

Chapter Three

Martin was smiling as she opened the door. "I thought you must have forgotten I was coming and gone out," he told her, moving forward to kiss her lightly.

"Sorry," she said, lying instinctively. "I was in the bathroom." Her body leaned away from him, as she spoke, in an involuntary movement of evasion which she picked up even as it happened.

He was flushed, his firm, smoothly shaven skin freshly colored after walking in the cold spring air. Taking off his overcoat he handed it to her, showing her the bottle of wine he carried.

"How does that grab you? It's a very good vintage."

"Lovely," she smiled, hanging his coat up. "I'm afraid lunch is going to be a little late."

Martin looked at her with amusement, his eyes

dancing. "I get it—you overslept, didn't you? You look pretty hectic. Have you been rushing around trying to make up for lost time?"

Nicola put a trembling hand to her hot face. She looked hectic, did she? Well, she wasn't surprised to be told so, but she was furious with herself.

"Something like that," she said, in as cool a tone as she could manage. "Would you like to open the wine now? I haven't got anything else to drink, I'm afraid, except some red wine."

"How long will lunch be?"

She glanced at her watch. "Another hour, Martin. I'm sorry."

"Then why don't we have some coffee?" He was always so calm and easygoing. She looked at him with warm appreciation. Martin was a man you could depend on, a man who wouldn't rush off to dangerous places on the other side of the world and leave you aching with misery, not knowing if he was alive or dead.

"I'll make it now," she promised, moving into the kitchen with Martin behind her.

"It looks as if it might rain," he said as she plugged in the percolator. "I'm beginning to wonder if we're going to have a spring at all this year."

"It has been rather cold," she agreed absently, half of her attention given to any hint of sound from the bedroom. Would Steve stay in there? Should she take this opportunity to explain to Martin that they were not alone in the flat? It might be better for her to tell him now rather than wait on tenterhooks to see if Steve betrayed his presence.

She knew she ought to do that but Nicola disliked

confrontations, arguments, angry voices. She wasn't sure how Martin would react and she half hoped that Steve would not make it necessary for her to tell Martin anything.

"You should get quite a good price for this place when you sell," Martin told her, looking around the kitchen.

Nicola nodded. She would have liked to ask him to keep his voice down but she could only do that if she told him why she wanted to be quiet.

"How much did you pay for it?" he asked as she got down the coffee cups.

She looked around, frowning. "Twenty thousand but prices have shot up since, of course."

Martin looked immaculate. He always did, his clothes conservative but carefully chosen to match his image. He had explained to her that his clients liked to be sure their money was in good hands. They liked their stockbroker to be safe, trustworthy, reliable. Martin was all those things. He was everything Nicola felt a husband should be. He was the opposite of Steve.

"You haven't got a date fixed for the divorce hearing yet?" he asked.

Her hand shook as she switched off the percolator and Martin looked at her in surprise. "You're very edgy this morning."

"Sorry," she said, trying to smile. "The divorce won't be heard for ages. There's a long waiting list, my solicitor tells me. I'll have to wait until my name gets to the top." She hesitated. Now was the moment to tell him that Steve was back in London. Moistening her lips, she tried to get the words out, but she was not certain of her voice. She needed time to think, work out how to bring him into the conversation. She had never been able to talk to Martin about Steve. She was half afraid of what she might betray if she said anything.

Swinging away, she began to pour the coffee, watching the black stream of liquid as it filled the cups.

"Darling, could you press my pants before I get dressed?" Steve's casual voice made her jump ten feet into the air. Scalding coffee sprayed over her hand. She put the pot down with a crash, gasping and trembling.

Martin stood up in a reflex action, his face torn between concern for her and surprise at Steve's sudden arrival, his head swinging from one to the other and his frown growing as he absorbed the fact that Steve was wearing nothing but a short robe which he had only tied loosely.

Steve was beside her before Martin had moved, taking hold of her hand and thrusting it under the cold tap. After a moment he turned off the water and inspected her reddened skin, his expression concerned. "How does it feel now?"

She pulled her hand away and put it behind her back like a child, her lower lip sulky. Her eye moved nervously to Martin. He was staring at them. "This is my husband," Nicola mumbled, very flushed.

Steve ran his blue eyes over Martin in a casual assessment before giving him a crooked smile. "We had better introduce ourselves, as Nicola has fallen down on the job. I'm Steve Howard." He did not offer his hand although Martin, always polite and conscious of the social niceties, had moved forward with his own hand held out.

Martin let his hand fall, embarrassment written all over him. "Martin Eastwood," he responded.

"I imagined you must be," Steve drawled. "Of course, it is possible she has half a dozen ardent suitors but somehow I don't see Nicky in the role of femme fatale."

Nicola looked at him irritably. "Thank you," she muttered.

He crooked a mocking eyebrow. "Oh, would you rather I saw you as one? Sorry. I'll try, if you like." His blue eyes drifted down over her in her jeans and discreet shirt. "You don't quite look the part, though. Something in clinging black would be more appropriate."

"Oh, shut up," Nicola said, her face scarlet.

Steve looked at Martin, who was staring, his mouth open. "So you want to marry my wife," Steve said pleasantly.

Martin had grown very red. This scene was not going the way Martin felt it should—the way, no doubt, he had imagined his first meeting with Nicola's ex-husband would be.

He had a vague grasp of the fact that Steve was getting at him. "I didn't know you were here," he said, stammering slightly.

Steve looked under his lashes at Nicola, the oblique mockery deepening in his eyes. "Oh, Nicky, you didn't tell him," he said sweetly, pretended reproach in his tone.

Martin had made up his mind about Steve. He did not like him. Keeping his eyes on Nicola he said with all the calm he could muster, "What's he doing here, Nicola?"

"We *are* still married," Steve pointed out before she could answer. "The deed to this flat is in my name."

Deciding to ignore that, Martin kept his eyes on Nicola's disturbed face. "You should have warned me," he said.

"I'm sorry." She knew she should have warned him. She wished she hadn't been such a coward. "I was going to," she explained rather limply.

Steve picked up the coffee cup nearest to him and sipped some of the black coffee. "Just what I need," he told Martin, who looked at him as if he hoped the coffee would choke him.

Moving toward Nicola, Martin lowered his voice to a confidential, chiding murmur. "He shouldn't be here, Nicola. Surely you realize that? It could prejudice your divorce."

"I've told him that," she said. "He doesn't take any notice."

"Oh, doesn't he?" Martin bristled, swinging around to face Steve, who went on drinking coffee, his blue eyes very bright. "Now, look here," Martin began aggressively.

"No, you look," Steve said, putting down the cup. "Of the two of us, I have more right in this flat than you do, so mind your own business."

"Nicola wants you to leave," Martin informed him. "Don't you, darling?"

"I've told him I do."

"You see?" Martin said, turning back to Steve. "You heard what she said."

"I heard," Steve agreed indifferently.

"Then you had better go," Martin pointed out. "You can't insist on staying if Nicola wants you to leave."

"Why not?"

Martin was staggered. "Why not?" he repeated. "Well, obviously . . ."

"Obviously what?" Steve was enjoying himself, leaning against the draining board, his long body relaxed and at ease, his eyes watching Martin like a cat with a mouse.

"Nicola has told you . . ."

"I never listen to anything a woman says," Steve drawled with enjoyment. "If you do, you're a fool. They never mean half of what they say. You should have worked that out for yourself by now. You have to read between the lines with them. It's a bit like doing the crossword in the papers—half guesswork, half an informed suspicion."

Martin had the look of a man about to explode. He squared himself, his elegantly clad body tense. "If you won't go, I'll have to throw you out," he told Steve.

Nicola closed her eyes.

Steve laughed. The sound of his laughter told her that that was precisely what Steve had been angling for—the offer of violence. It could only have one outcome. Martin was slim and active but he hadn't a chance against Steve's powerful, muscled strength.

"You and whose army?" Steve asked him softly, not shifting from his casual stance.

Martin went at him with a furious gasp. Steve moved too fast for Nicola to see what happened but the next second Martin was flat on his back, a hand to his nose, making muffled gasps of pain.

Nicola ran to kneel beside him, full of contrition and distress. "You're a brute," she yelled over her shoulder at Steve as she tried to see what damage he had done to Martin's nose.

Steve strolled away, stepping over Martin's feet with composure on his way to the door. "Don't forget I want my pants pressed," he told her as he vanished.

"My nose," Martin grunted, still clasping it.

"Oh, dear," Nicola groaned, looking at him in flushed, anxious disturbance. "I am sorry, Martin."

Martin gingerly removed his hand. His nose seemed perfectly normal, except that it was rather red. "He's got a fist like a steamhammer," he said sulkily. "Anyway, he took me by surprise. He jumped at me before I was ready."

Nicola was suddenly irritated with them both. Martin looked like a little boy who had lost a fight.

"I'll be ready for him next time," he said and Nicola got up, stiff with impatience.

"Don't be ridiculous. What good would that do?"

"It will do me a lot of good," Martin said. "I owe him a good punch in the nose, remember."

Steve had left his trousers over a chair. Nicola picked them up absent-mindedly. They were very crumpled. What had happened to his other luggage? she wondered. Did he have to leave it behind to get away? It wouldn't be the first time he had lost a whole wardrobe. Once before he had had to abandon all his belongings to escape with a whole skin.

Martin slowly got to his feet, staring at her as she

let down the ironing board from the cupboard which held it. "What are you doing?"

"Pressing his pants," Nicola said, getting out the iron and plugging it in.

"You're not going to do that for him, are you?" He sounded so furious she looked around at him.

"He can't wear these as they are. He must have slept in them for days."

"Too bad," Martin muttered. He switched off the iron, his expression black with temper. "Let him get someone else to do it. You aren't his slave."

Nicola looked at the creased trousers. "No," she said. "I'm not, am I?" He was right. She hadn't been thinking properly.

"Who does he think he is?" Martin said rhetorically.

"Good question." She had often asked herself that in the past.

"He's an arrogant devil," Martin said, his lips tight.

"I couldn't agree with you more."

"I had no idea. You said he was difficult but I didn't realize how much so."

"He's a brute." She looked at Martin, her face warm. "Your poor nose." She leaned toward him, kissing it gently. "How does it feel now?"

Martin slid his arms around her slender waist and kissed her lips. "It's getting better all the time."

The door opened and Steve lounged there in a shirt, his long legs very brown. Nicola instinctively jumped away from Martin and got a hard unsmiling look from the blue eyes.

"Where are my pants?"

"She isn't pressing them," Martin told him, but he said it with a wary eye on Steve, poised to move back if Steve moved an inch.

"If she hasn't pressed them in five minutes, I'll have yours," Steve informed him silkily. He smiled as he said it, the reasonable smile of the tiger regarding the tethered goat which it would claim any minute, then he walked out again, letting the door slam.

Martin said something Nicola ignored. She plugged the iron back in and began pressing the trousers.

"I'll break his neck if he comes near me again," Martin told her but he didn't try to stop her.

"He's got a horrible temper," Nicola said as she watched the steam hissing up.

"He looks as if he has," agreed Martin, straightening his tie with one hand. "What is he doing in London?"

She nodded toward the paper. "That's his story—the lead. He was thrown out by the government there. They said they would shoot him if he went back."

"I'll buy him a plane ticket," Martin muttered, picking up the paper and beginning to read. His face changed. Nicola finished pressing the trousers while he made his way through the story.

She heard him swallow. "I didn't realize," he said under his breath.

Nicola met his eyes. "You hadn't heard about it?"

"Oh, they had the story in my paper but not in this detail."

She nodded. "I think Steve was the only reporter

in the area." He would be, she thought. Typical of him to be on the spot when something like that happened.

"It must have been murder," Martin said, and she began to laugh hysterically.

Looking at her in impatient bewilderment, he asked, "What's so funny about that?"

Her laughter died, as if it had been switched off. "Nothing," she said wearily. "Not a thing."

Martin did not understand her, she could see. He was looking as if he thought she needed her head examined. "You're upset," he told her gently. "No wonder you looked distraught when you opened the door. Why on earth didn't you tell me he was here?"

"I didn't want any trouble," she said, and that was funny too. She couldn't help laughing but her laughter had that edge of hysteria which bordered on tears.

Martin looked at her grimly. "Well, you got it anyway," he said, and she nodded.

"I did, didn't I? There's always trouble when Steve Howard is around. All over the world people say, 'Oh, no!' when they see him flying into the country. They know that where he goes, trouble follows."

Her trembling voice cut off as Steve came back into the room. He had shaved now, his tanned face smooth and still slightly damp.

He didn't say a word, just took his trousers and slid into them, ignoring Martin and Nicola.

Martin looked at him with embarrassed concern. "I've just read your story," he said, clearing his throat. "Terrible."

Steve pretended not to understand him. "Is it? Well, the subs will take a hatchet to my best work, you know."

Martin struggled to be polite. "I meant that the news was terrible," he expanded. "A shocking story—it must have been a nightmare for you."

Steve shot Nicola a hard, querying look, as though asking her something. She met his stare with surprised bewilderment, then, as he said brusquely, "Yes, it was," she realized that he had wondered if she had told Martin about his nightmare. Steve hated to reveal anything of himself, particularly anything anyone might read as a weakness.

"When will that lunch be ready?" he asked, turning to her, and Nicola exclaimed, "The chicken!" She flew to the oven to inspect it. An appetizing aroma wafted out into the room and Steve sighed deeply.

"I'm starving. I could eat that all by myself."

The phone rang in the living room and Steve glanced around. "That will be for me, I expect. I left this number." He went out and Martin watched as Nicola tested the vegetables.

"Nicola," he said slowly, his tone thoughtful.

She looked up. "Yes?"

Martin was looking at her very oddly. "You haven't . . ." He broke off, his face rather confused, coloring. "How long has he been here?"

"He was here when I got back last night," she told him, not getting the point.

"He's been here all night?" His tone made it clear then; she felt herself going pink.

"Yes, and before you ask me, he slept in the bed but I slept on the couch." She could not help the slight acidity with which she said that. Martin was looking at her accusingly and Nicola did not like it. He had no right to look at her like that.

He relaxed. "Oh."

"Yes, oh," she snapped, and Martin tried to placate her, giving her a coaxing smile.

"You don't still fancy him then?" That was a very heavy attempt at humor and she wasn't responding to it.

Her face cold, she said, "No, I don't fancy him."

Steve loomed up in the doorway, catching the words, and giving her a hard stare, his brows meeting above his eyes. He did not speak to her, however; he addressed Martin with brisk courtesy, a threat still lurking in the clear blue of his eyes.

"I'm expecting some people from the office any minute, but there isn't any whiskey in the place. Would you do me a small favor? There's an off-license on the corner. I'd be grateful if you would go down there and get me a bottle of whiskey. I'd go myself but I ought to stay here in case they arrive."

Martin looked to Nicola for guidance, and she shrugged. Apparently deciding that as Steve seemed to be ignoring the incident he might as well, too, he picked up his coat, departing like a lamb. Steve glanced at Nicola who was straining the carrots, her attention fixed on what she was doing.

"I can see why you picked him," he drawled.

Nicola pretended not to hear that. She was not going to talk about Martin to him. She was still angry with Steve for the way he had behaved earlier. He had had no business taunting Martin into a fight which Steve knew very well he would win with one hand tied behind his back. Martin led a very sedentary life. He was fit enough for the life-style he enjoyed but Steve was a much tougher proposition. He had to be, his job demanded it. He had learned to look after himself in a rough school. He had the alert instincts of a jungle animal.

"What turns you on?" Steve demanded, watching her closely. "His smooth manner or his looks?"

"Martin is nothing like you," Nicola said coldly. "That's what turns me on."

"I thought it might be something like that." She had hoped to prick his thick skin but she could see that she had only amused him instead. He was grinning and looking as if he liked that idea.

"At least this time I shall be getting a husband when I marry, not just a flying lover," Nicola muttered, turning away from him.

She wasn't looking at him as she spoke and she hadn't heard him move. When his voice came just behind her it made her jump, her eyes opening wide, startled and alarmed.

"For the next week I'm not flying anywhere," he said, his voice deep and husky, then his mouth burrowed into the back of her neck and her pulse went crazy, her breath hurting as she tried to drag air into her lungs.

"Don't do that," she whispered breathlessly.

His arms had gone around her waist, his hands moving just below the uplift of her breast.

"I've been waiting for this for months," he said, his kiss sliding to her ear.

She pushed at his hands, wriggling in the cage of his embrace, trapped between him and the sink. "What do you think I am? You must despise me if you think you can just fly in and out of my life like a homing pigeon. If you wanted me, you wouldn't have stayed away so long. The only thing that matters to you is your job."

His hands shifted upward and she felt those long fingers closing over her breasts and her pulse accelerated once more. This warm possession sent waves of excitement pulsing through her.

"Nicky," he whispered, his lips moving softly against her neck again.

She knew what he was doing. The temptation of those experienced hands, the teasing mouth, did not need any explanation. Nicola shut her weakening mind to what he was offering. She reminded herself of the empty nights, the lonely days, he had given her in the past.

"Will you leave me alone?" She broke away, turning to face him and he watched her intently, staring into her angry eyes with a frown.

"We're still married, Nicky," he reminded.

"We've never been married!" It had not been marriage as she understood the word.

"Don't talk nonsense," he said impatiently, shifting his stance in an uneasy movement. He had always avoided discussions of this sort. He had not wanted her to bring it all out into the open. He wanted to keep things light between them. That left him free to fly away whenever he chose without feeling that he left any problems behind him. Steve ran from involvement. He felt trapped when she tried to make him admit that their life-style was no longer going to work. Marriage was a trap; that was how he saw it. So he had tried to be married and yet free, but Nicola was not prepared to share him with his job.

"We went through a legal ceremony," she threw back. "But as far as real marriage was concerned, you never even considered it. You put a ring on my finger, took me to bed and then went back to what you really enjoy—your job."

"You're being ridiculous," he argued, his face darkening as he listened. "You can't expect me to take that seriously."

"I don't," she agreed scathingly. "You've never taken me seriously."

"You're wrong." He moved nearer, a harsh light in his eyes. "I take you very seriously."

"No," she denied. "To you I'm just a woman you like going to bed with."

"If that was true, I'd never have married you at all," he said furiously. "Do you think you were the first girl I'd ever wanted to take to bed?"

Jealously, she muttered, "I'm sure I wasn't."

"I didn't marry any of the others."

"Maybe they had more sense than I did. Maybe they wouldn't have you."

"Maybe I didn't ask any of them," he told her, his eyes growing cold.

"I wish you hadn't asked me!"

The coldness deepened, hardening all the lines of his face. "Thank you."

"If I'd realized you didn't intend to take our marriage seriously, I would have turned you down. I want a normal marriage with a husband who comes home to me every night." Her voice had begun to shake, she was afraid she was going to cry. She tried to steady herself, biting on her inner lip. "I want a house, children . . ." Her voice broke. She couldn't finish; it hurt too much.

He moved restlessly, watching her as she brushed the back of her hand over her eyes. When he moved closer and tried to put an arm around her, though, she pushed him away, giving him a bitter look.

"I don't want you touching me!"

He fell back, taking a deep breath. "Why are you in such a rush? There will be plenty of time for children. But if you want one that badly we could have one right away."

"While you go back to Africa, leaving me to have it on my own? No, thank you. I want a baby, but not like that. I'm not planning on a one-parent family."

"Neither am I," he retorted. "I'm intending to give up foreign reporting one day. I'll get a desk job in London."

Nicola's breath stilled. She looked at him sharply, searching his face. "When?"

He grimaced. "Sometime."

Her body sagged. He was talking at random, making vague promises. He didn't mean them. Steve liked the way his life was arranged. He had the best of both worlds—an exciting job which gave him plenty of travel, glamor, the danger he loved—and a wife waiting in London for him whenever he chose to come back to her.

"If they don't send you home in a coffin first," she said with biting rage.

Steve gave a sudden grin, reckless amusement in his eyes. "They'll have their work cut out."

He thought he was indestructible, did he? Nicola wished she could believe he was—she looked at the all-too-human vulnerability of his amused face and hated him. One bullet could stop that laughter forever. His lean body was a beautifully streamlined machine, the taut brown skin smooth over those strong bones, the mind behind the blue eyes quick and clever. Unlike machines, though, Steve was flesh and blood.

"Well, I'm not waiting around to find out," she told him with bitterness. "You go on risking your life for as long as you like, but count me out. I've had enough." She could not face any more of the interminable waiting, worrying, the nights without sleep and the days when her nerves jumped every time the phone rang.

Steve pushed his hands down into his pockets, watching her with an unreadable expression. "And when you've divorced me, you plan to marry your stockbroker?"

"I haven't made up my mind what I'm going to do." Martin was always talking as though she had said she would marry him when the divorce was through, but she had never committed herself. Martin took too much for granted. Men always did, she thought, her face impatient. They seemed to think it was up to them to make decisions and all a woman had to do was fall in line obediently.

"How long has it been going on?" Steve demanded.

She didn't like the way he phrased that, or the narrowed glare of his eyes. "I met Martin a few months ago," she said coldly.

He laughed, a vicious mimicry of amusement, his mouth twisting and his blue eyes scathing. "The minute my back was turned . . ."

She interrupted that sentence with a gasp of fury. "I'd already started the divorce proceedings, and if you turn your back, you can't be surprised if I walk away. Did you think I enjoyed living like a widow? How much time did you actually spend with me after we were married? It's surprising I remembered what you looked like. If I hadn't had a few photos, I would have thought you were a mirage."

"So you scouted around for someone else, did you?"

Flushing, she snapped, "No, I met Martin purely by accident."

"Oh, of course," he sneered.

"It was! I was at a party when we met. I was on my own and so was he . . ."

"What a touching story," Steve interrupted. "I've heard it before, though. Adultery always starts like that."

"I told you," she broke out breathlessly. "We haven't . . ."

"You told me," he agreed, watching her with a harsh frown. "But how do I know you told me the truth?"

"I don't happen to believe in . . ." she began, and he laughed unpleasantly.

"How high-minded. Doesn't a lot depend on your definition of the word adultery? Where do you draw the line, Nicola?" He moved closer and looked down at her, his face hard. "Does he kiss you?"

She looked away, her eyelids fluttering.

Steve caught her face between his hands. "How does he kiss you?" he asked thickly. "Like this, Nicola?" His mouth moved sensually against her lips, parting them, probing between them. She felt his fingers unbuttoning her shirt and moving under it, the cool tips of them gently sliding over the flat plane of her midriff until he was cupping one breast. "Does he do that, my darling?" Steve whispered against her trembling mouth.

There was a tremulous feeling deep inside her and her pulses beat fiercely. She couldn't answer, her mouth too dry to speak.

Steve's hand moved around to her back. She felt him unclip her bra and she tried to break away. His hand closed on her waist, holding her. "Oh, no," he said. "Not yet, my darling. We haven't finished our little experiment. You haven't told me enough yet."

She felt his fingers brushing gently over the warm white flesh he had exposed and her eyes closed helplessly. She was breathing fast, her lips parted on a stifled moan.

"Has he had your clothes off yet?" The terse question broke into her weak surrender and she shuddered.

"No, no, no." There was mounting pain in her voice.

Steve cupped her breast, bending to touch his lips to the hard pink nipple. "I hope he hasn't," he muttered, his breath warm on her body. "Like most women you have a positive genius for telling lies with your eyes wide open and a look of indignant innocence on your face."

"I'm not lying, but if I wanted to sleep with Martin, I would," she said bitterly.

"I'd kill you if you did," Steve said, with raw rage threaded through his voice. He straightened and brought his mouth down on hers with demanding fire, the force of the kiss driving her head back, her throat stretched and aching. She felt his hand caress her neck, push into her hair and wind among the black strands. He pulled her head back even further and the kiss became violent, cruel, a punishing possession which sapped all her will to fight him.

The jangle of the doorbell snapped them both out of their passionate trance. Steve lifted his head, breathing sharply, a dark red color in his face and leaping desire in his eyes. Nicola swayed, moistening her bruised lips with her tongue. The pressure of Steve's mouth had driven them back upon her teeth, and she felt the tiny soreness, grimacing.

The bell rang again. "That will be Martin with the whiskey," Nicola whispered in an unsteady voice.

"You'd better let him in then, hadn't you?" Steve released her and ran his derisive eye over her open shirt, the firm pale breasts he had been caressing. "You had better tidy yourself up before you do, though. We wouldn't want your boyfriend to know I'd been sharing your favors."

Her hand flew out in an involuntary gesture. The

slap of it as it connected with his face surprised them both. Steve stared as she jumped back, her eyes enormous. Putting one hand to his cheek he grimaced. "You'll pay for that later," he promised silkily.

She turned away, trembling even more, and hurriedly did up her bra and then her shirt before she went to open the door.

Chapter Four

Martin thrust the bottle of whiskey into her hands. He was looking rather annoyed and at once broke out, "I've been thinking. I can't stay to lunch now, can I? If he refuses to leave, we must go. Why don't we have lunch elsewhere? We'll eat out at a restaurant."

She was tempted to agree out of sheer defiance, but the heated trolley in the kitchen was full of food she had spent the morning getting ready, and if they did go out, she knew Steve would never bother to eat any of that food. That was one thing she had learned about him during their strange, sporadic marriage. Steve was very vague about meals. He might make himself a sandwich but she knew he wouldn't dream of serving the meal she had prepared.

"I can't," she told Martin. "I'll have to stay." After all, this was her home. Why should she let Steve drive her out of it? She did not quite trust him, anyway. She wanted to keep an eye on him while he was in the flat. Seeing Martin's frown, she added, "He *is* expecting people. I'm not going out and leaving them all here. Who knows what sort of orgy they might have?" She could imagine coming home to find the flat full of noisy newspapermen, the air full of cigarette smoke and the smell of whiskey. She knew those parties. Once they got talking about their job they forgot everything else.

Martin had begun to look very sulky. That calm manner of his did not tend to the sort of savage temper Steve could fly into, but it did produce the occasional fit of the sulks. "It puts me in a very false position," he said. "You aren't changing your mind, are you?"

"What about?" She was thinking about the lunch which was going to be ruined if someone did not eat it soon and she did not get his drift.

"The divorce," he said, and Nicola gave him an angry look, going rather pink.

"No, I'm not." She paused, and decided that that was not definite or vehement enough, so she said, "Certainly not!" She hoped that left no room for doubt.

"You're very complacent about letting him stay here," Martin said with more shrewdness than she liked.

"Nothing of the kind," she retorted. "I've told him to go over and over again. He takes no notice."

It was like talking to a brick wall to try to get Steve to take any notice if he chose not to do so.

"You could make him go," Martin informed her and she looked at him scathingly.

"Oh, yes? What do I do? Pick him up and throw him out? You try it." Her tone made Martin turn very red and she was apologetic as she met his eyes. He was hurt. Although she had not actually said so, she had implied that Martin couldn't stand up to Steve. The sting in that implication was, of course, that after what had happened between the two men earlier, Martin was angrily aware that he couldn't.

"He's a nasty piece of work," Martin said, almost as though he was blaming her for that, as though she had deliberately produced Steve out of a hat. "I can't see what you saw in him."

"Neither can I," she lied, her eyes shifting away and her mouth wry. She sighed, shrugging her shoulders. "I'm sorry to spoil your day for you, Martin, but I suppose you're right. You had better go."

He lingered, chewing on his lower lip. "I'm worried about leaving you here alone with him."

"I'll be okay," she said reassuringly.

Martin did not quite meet her eyes. "I don't like it," he said, and she knew perfectly well what was in his mind. Martin was far too conventional to come out with it but he was worrying about the idea of her being alone in the flat with her husband in case Steve talked her into bed.

"I can manage him," she said, with less truth than optimism.

"Can you?" Martin clearly did not believe her. "Sure you don't want me to stick around?"

"No," she said. "Steve's my problem."

Martin gave her a look then opened the door, his face blank. "If you want me, you know where I live," he said, stalking out. Martin was not the sort of person to make a noisy protest. He was too conscious of his dignity. It came over, though, that he was angry with her. What also came over was that Martin was less deeply wounded than he was annoyed. The hurt was to his self-respect rather than his heart.

There had always been some sort of unreality about her relationship with Martin. They had been too nice to each other, too careful, too polite. She had told herself that that was because Martin was a nice, polite man, but it had been more than that.

Martin had never been in love with her. Love would have been more urgent, more demanding. Martin liked her, he found her attractive. He felt she would suit his life-style. He had had a number of sound reasons for asking her to marry him, but love had not been one of them. It was just that Martin was conventional enough to believe love must be the only reason for marrying anyone, so he had pretended feelings he didn't really have.

Holding the bottle of whiskey, she walked slowly back into the kitchen. Steve was leaning against the sink, his arms folded, and a harsh frown on his face.

The blue eyes fixed her. "Well, where is he?"

"Gone," Nicola said, putting down the whiskey.

Steve began to grin and she resented that. Today she was ready to resent a lot of things.

"You can take that grin off your face," she yelled, turning on him like a wildcat.

"Don't shout at me," Steve said, the grin vanishing.

"I'll shout all I want to," Nicola informed him. "Who do you think you are?"

"I think I'm your husband."

"Not for long," she said with bitter satisfaction.

A hard, cold expression came into his face. "Then I'd better make the most of the time that's left, hadn't I?"

"You're not touching me," she said, a thread of panic in her voice as he moved toward her.

"You sound scared, Nicola," he taunted, smiling tightly. "Why is that? What are you scared of? That you might enjoy it, by any chance?"

She had backed involuntarily away from him, trembling, but now she stood her ground, her chin lifted and her eyes burning with anger.

"I'm not scared at all," she lied.

He laughed, so close to her now that their bodies almost touched, looking down at her with mockery and cold appraisal. "Liar," he whispered in a low, intimate voice. He lifted a hand and touched the side of her neck. "What's that?" The little pulse beneath his finger beat faster. "A dead giveaway," he told her, his mouth twisting.

"Get your hand off me," she said shakily.

His fingers caressed her throat, wakening more pulses, and that made her angrier than ever. He had one easy way to get under her skin and he knew it. If he had any principles, he wouldn't be doing this. Hadn't he hurt her enough?

"You're a selfish, self-satisfied brute," she said with such passion that his hand dropped away from her.

She took advantage of his disbelief at her tone. Meeting his stare, she said, "How dare you criticize me for dating Martin? How dare you walk in here and expect to be welcomed with open arms after all this time? What do you think marriage is? This has never been your home. You've treated it like a hotel. I won't describe how you've treated me, but you're never doing it again."

"What do *you* think marriage is?" he retorted with a contemptuous stare. "Or don't you remember the words 'for better for worse?' I seem to recall you saying them."

"I wasn't expecting the worst so soon," Nicola muttered. "I had no idea that you married me with every intention of walking out on me almost at once."

He shifted irritably. "I didn't walk out. I was sent on a story. It's my job. You knew what my job was when we got married."

"I didn't know it was going to mean we never saw each other."

"I couldn't take you with me, it wasn't safe," he said, frowning. "It was too risky, Nicky."

"If it was risky, you could have given me the option. You didn't, did you? You didn't discuss it with me. You just flew off and left me."

"I missed you," he murmured, looking at her through his lashes, a coaxing little smile appearing on his face.

She was not going to let him wheedle her. She

turned away, her face cold. "The lunch is ready," she said, her tone ending the conversation.

"Blast the lunch," he roared, slamming out.

Nicola went on with serving the meal, her eyes grim. When it was ready, she called him and after a pause he came, his strong face expressionless now. During the interval, she got the feeling, he had been reviewing their argument. As they ate he kept shooting her quick, assessing looks, but he said nothing.

Only when they had finished their meal did he say, "I sometimes suspect you want a home more than you want a husband. You have a very fixed idea of what marriage should be."

Nicola didn't answer. She had been an only child, brought up in a very quiet, contented home life, and she couldn't deny that she had wanted to reproduce that happy atmosphere with Steve. Her parents had both died before she met Steve. For some years she had lived alone in London's lonely wasteland and perhaps she had expected marriage to give her back the warm background she had grown up in. She had no family and few friends. She only knew she needed to belong.

"I just want my husband with me all the time, not hundreds of miles away," she muttered.

"You make points like someone hammering in nails," he muttered.

"I hope you're getting them, then."

"You'll get something, in a minute," he threatened, and she gave him a defiant stare.

"You're so civilized. Faced with any argument, you react by making threats."

"That wasn't a threat, it was a promise," he said, his eyes dark with temper, getting up in a violent movement to move around to her.

The doorbell rang as she leaped up, sending her chair crashing to the floor. Steve swore under his breath. "Teddy," he said, spinning to stride away. Nicola picked up her chair with shaking hands. She heard the editor of the paper talking at the front door, heard Steve answering him in a calm and level tone which revealed nothing of the temper she had seen a moment ago.

Steve walked back into the room with Teddy at his heels, beaming over the rims of his spectacles. "Nicola, nice to see you."

"Hello, Mr. Wiseman," she said politely, giving him a pretense of a smile.

He was a large, untidy man whose clothes always looked as though he slept in them. Nobody ran around after Teddy Wiseman to make sure his suit was pressed. He shambled as he walked, his body rolling from side to side, but when things got heated up around the office, nobody could move faster. Teddy only really lived when a deadline was coming closer and his particular brand of urgent energy was required. Then he straightened up, his whole manner changing. That adrenaline was a necessary part of his job and it was probably all that kept Teddy from lapsing into a total stupor.

"Seen the story this man of yours brought back? Good stuff, isn't it? He's a miracle man. I like to have a scoop now and then—keeps us on our toes, eh, Steve?"

"Sure," Steve said, collecting the whiskey and glasses.

Nicola got an odd idea. She felt Steve was trying to steer Teddy away. He had a furtive, evasive look.

"He's told you, has he?" Teddy asked, and she felt Steve's uneasiness increase.

"Later," he said, grabbing Teddy's arm to pull him into the living room.

Teddy did not go. He gave Nicola a cheerful grin. "Try to talk him into it."

"Into what?" she asked, and he threw Steve a quick look.

"You haven't told her?"

"Not yet," Steve said curtly. "I haven't made up my own mind yet. Until I do, I'm not discussing it."

"Discussing what?" Nicola asked, and both men ignored her. They talked across her as though she was a child. She could have screamed.

"Shouldn't Nicola have a say in it?" Teddy asked him.

"No," Steve said, leaving no room for argument.

"In what?" Nicola asked. Maybe if she said it often enough, one of them might see fit to enlighten her as to what they were talking about.

"Nothing," Steve said. "Teddy, come into the living room and have some whiskey while Nicola does the washing up."

That puts me in my place, she thought. I do the domestic chores while they drink the whiskey. Who says women are emancipated? They may have made a law about it but it isn't worth the paper it's written on until it's women who drink the whiskey while men do the chores. She looked at Steve, trying to imagine him in an apron, but failed. It just wasn't his scene. It wasn't just women who had been conditioned to see themselves in certain roles. Men had, too. Steve had a vital individuality which sprang from his certainty about his role in life. He didn't have to think about it. He was sexually confident and it blazed out of those blue eyes.

Teddy detached his arm from Steve's guiding hand. "With all due respect, I think Nicola ought to be involved in your thinking," he said with a quick smile at her which she read all too easily. Teddy wasn't speaking as a representative of the male sex now. He was speaking as someone with an axe to grind. He was enrolling Nicola on his team. He wanted her to bring her influence to bear on Steve in whatever he wanted Steve to do.

"Well, I don't," Steve muttered, but he was too late.

"I've offered Steve the job of Deputy Foreign News Editor," Teddy told her.

Nicola stiffened, her eyes flying to Steve. He grimaced, impatience in every inch of him.

"I haven't decided yet," he said, frowning.

"Now," Teddy said, happily sure that she was going to help him persuade Steve, "what do you say to that, Nicola?"

She looked away from Steve, her face icy. "That it's up to Steve," she said. "It's his job."

For a moment there was total silence. Steve stared at her in what appeared to be stupefied disbelief. Teddy's face dropped like a stone.

"Oh," he said, ludicrously discomfited.

Nicola turned and walked back to the sink to get on with the washing up and after a moment she heard the two men depart, closing the door behind them. She scrubbed viciously at a saucepan, her teeth clenched together.

Nothing had altered. Faced with the threatened divorce, Steve was still not prepared to give up his way of life. What point would there be in trying to change his mind? She had pleaded, begged, argued and cried in the past. Not anymore. She was going to follow his example and just go ahead with her own plans, ignoring their effect on him.

The doorbell rang again, and from the living room Steve yelled, "Get that, would you, Nicky?"

"Get it yourself," she yelled back, banging saucepans down as she dried them.

There was a stunned silence, then she heard him going to the front door. Nicola rarely had visitors. Her social life had never been ultra active. She was too shy. At parties she tended to sit in a corner and watch; she didn't have much to say to strangers. It always seemed such hard work hunting for small talk. She had, in fact, had more visitors at the flat this morning than she normally got during a week. Steve had a lot of friends, and whenever he had been in London they had descended in a horde. Nicola hadn't got to know any of them very well. She was too silent. She had found her role confined to going around refilling glasses, offering sandwiches, smiling shyly.

For the first time in her life she was facing herself and the way she lived and not liking either very much. From the very beginning, she realized, she had unconsciously been presenting Steve with an image of her which had affected the way he responded to her. His behavior had been conditioned by her own.

She heard him talking, heard men's deep cheerful voices, the sound of footsteps. "Joanne," Steve said in a very different voice, the voice he reserved for the opposite sex, and someone laughed. The door was shut but through it Nicola fancied she got waves of perfume. She glared at it. Joanne Hollis, she thought darkly. What's she doing here?

Joanne was one of the reporters. She got all the stories with a feminine angle. She also got a lot of the men. Joanne was a vibrant redhead with a taste for variety and come-hither green eyes. Nicola had rarely spoken to her but she had seen her swaying through the building in very tight skirts and so much perfume that after she had vanished it hung around in the air stifling everyone.

Nicola flung the saucepans into their cupboard. The clatter brought an odd little silence from the other room. Then the voices resumed rather more loudly.

Steve appeared, closing the kitchen door behind him, eyeing Nicola with wary uncertainty. "I'll need some more glasses."

Nicola began to clean the sink, ignoring him.

"Why don't you come in and join us?" he suggested, hovering behind her.

"When they go, you go with them," she told him. She had no intention of walking in there in her jeans. She knew Joanne Hollis. Joanne advertised her sex appeal in neon lights and Nicola was not competing with her. Not yet, anyway, she thought. She had a lot of thinking to do first.

"I'm not arguing with you," Steve said, collecting some glasses and slamming out of the room.

Nicola finished tidying the kitchen then she quietly slipped off to her bedroom. She heard the voices rising and falling in the living room. Secure behind her bolted door, she stripped and hunted for something else to wear. A lot of things were going to change around here, she thought. And they might as well start changing now.

She had never seriously thought about herself before. Life rarely gives one time to stop and look at oneself from the outside. Day succeeds day in such battering rapidity. From childhood upward, the image inside one's head is formed like the growth of a pearl, so gradually that it isn't noticed.

Nicola thought about herself now, eyeing herself in the mirror with distaste. We are all partial, fragmentary, shifting, but that's not the image we have of ourselves. The self we project is a mixture of self-appraisal and the expectations of those we meet. People are constantly in motion, changing shape and form as you grasp them, yet we all tend to see ourselves as static.

Nicola had responded to Steve without knowing what she was doing, giving him back the image he desired. He had reacted to her in response to how she reacted to him. She saw that now. She had made no demands on him. She had yielded helplessly, allowing him to dictate the course of their relationship. If you're weak, you invite others to push you around.

Not anymore, she thought. She didn't know yet what she was or how she was going to shape her future, but she did know that it was going to be she who shaped it, not Steve or Martin or anyone else.

I've been pushed around long enough, she thought. From the mirror her own face stared back, the amber eyes fringed now with thick black false eyelashes, her mouth warm and glowing moistly, her delicately applied makeup lending color to her translucent skin. That's more like it, Nicola told the reflection.

She only had one dress which would make Steve sit up. She had bought it on impulse and left it hanging in her wardrobe because when she wore it, she got the sort of looks which made her feel uneasy. Some women like to be stared at like that. Nicola didn't. She usually wore clothes which made her safely invisible, using them as camouflage. But not today—today Nicola was going to make sure Steve knew she was there.

When she walked into the room, the voices stopped dead. The men half rose, looking at her with surprised interest.

Steve had been talking, a glass of whiskey between both hands, but he looked up, eyes widening. Nicola sauntered across the room under his sharp gaze, hoping she looked cool and casual.

"Hello," the men all murmured, and she smiled around the semi-circle, her glance avoiding Steve but lingering on Joanne Hollis.

"Hello, Joanne." Her smile had a fake sweetness.

"Hi," Joanne said, giving back the smile the way she had got it. Joanne was a man's woman. She had no time for other members of her sex and she had no friends at the newspaper, particularly among the secretarial staff, whom she treated with offhand contempt.

"What can I get you to drink?" Joe Fraser asked as she sat down beside him on the couch. He was one of the London-based reporters and was an old friend of Steve's. He knew Nicola quite well.

"Whatever you're drinking," she said, because there wasn't anything else, and when he handed her a small whiskey she sipped it, stifling a grimace of distaste.

"I'd like to shift over to foreign," Joanne said, leaning back and crossing her silkclad legs while Steve's blue eyes observed the graceful little movement with enjoyment.

Nicola sipped some more whiskey. If she didn't drink the stuff, she might toss it at Joanne.

"Tired of home news?" Steve was asking.

Joanne shrugged elegantly. She was wearing a white sweater cut so low it left nothing to the imagination and the shrug drew Steve's eyes from her legs upward. Joanne had a figure which curved in all the right places. She knew what to wear to draw attention to it, too.

"No way," Teddy said, his face sphinxlike.

Joanne gave him a coaxing little smile. "I'm sure I'd do well on the foreign team."

"Women who go in for foreign reporting have to be tough," Teddy said indulgently.

"I am tough," Joanne said, swallowing some whiskey in a casual fashion.

The men all laughed. Nicola didn't. She wasn't

viewing Joanne through the same rose-tinted spectacles they all wore. Joanne *was* tough. She might have a sexy figure, a pretty face and a flirtatious manner, but she couldn't hide from another woman the hardness in her green eyes, the acquisitive line of her mouth.

"Have you ever looked at the sort of women who work on foreign?" Teddy asked. "They can kick down doors."

"I don't need to kick them down," Joanne said demurely, and they all laughed.

"We're not talking about bedroom doors," one of the other men teased her.

Joanne looked at him through her lashes. "Charming," she purred.

"Teddy's right," Steve said. "The job doesn't suit women. Too much risk involved."

"Oh, I wasn't talking about turning war correspondent," she explained. "There are plenty of other jobs on foreign."

"Talking about jobs on foreign," Joe said, glancing across at Steve, "are you taking the deputy's job? David Wakeman leaves in a month's time, doesn't he?"

Teddy assumed a sweet smile. "Steve's thinking about it."

Steve looked at Nicola, who looked at her whiskey. She wasn't making much headway with it. A sip or two left far too much in the glass.

Joanne leaned over and put her hand on Steve's knee. "Oh, do take it," she pleaded girlishly.

Nicola looked at the other woman sideways, her teeth grating. Steve was smiling and looking into

Joanne's eyes. He didn't appear to object to the intimate way she was touching him, nor did he seem surprised by it. Steve had known Joanne for years. How well had he known her, though? Nicola wondered. He had never been communicative on the subject of his past relationships. Steve had a poker face when he chose to. He was wearing it now, under that smile. Nicola couldn't guess what was going on inside his black head.

"I'd need some persuading," Steve said, his lashes flicking toward Nicola, who ignored him.

"I'm very persuasive," Joanne told him, throwing all her sex appeal into the smoldering gaze of her eyes. "You're a natural for the job. You've been working out in the field for years and you wouldn't make any mistakes about the men you sent out to get a story."

"Or the women," Joe Fraser muttered under his breath. "She's flattering you, Steve. Watch out."

"I'm watching," Steve said with amusement. He looked as if he was enjoying Joanne's attentions.

Joe looked at Nicola thoughtfully. "I'm sure you want him to take the job."

"I don't care what he does," Nicola said, drinking some more of the whiskey and shuddering as the heat of it hit the back of her throat. Why do they drink this stuff? It tastes vile, she thought.

Steve was staring at her from across the room and their eyes met. "He's a free agent, he can do as he likes," she added.

There was a little silence. Joanne laughed softly under her breath. "I hope you're listening to this, Steve; I am," she said.

"Oh, so am I," Steve said through his teeth, with a recriminatory look flung toward Nicola which promised punishment when his friends had finally gone.

"I wish my wife took such an understanding attitude to my job," Peter Lewis said, brushing back his untidy hair. "She drives me nuts complaining about the hours I have to work. You must have a word with her, Nicola, teach her the secret of the perfect marriage."

Teddy Wiseman intervened hurriedly, "You shouldn't miss your chance of a London job, Steve. You can't stay out in the field forever. You have to give up that life one day, and the longer you leave it the harder you'll find it."

"I wasn't planning on coming home just yet," Steve said. "It gets into your blood. Life will seem pretty tame once I've come back to London for good."

Nicola looked into her whiskey. That says a lot for our marriage, doesn't it? she thought to herself. Tame and far from being an irresistible lure.

Joanne gave Steve one of her smoldering smiles. "You ought to be planning on an executive career. In your position, I would. You know you can't just walk into an editorship—you have to work your way up, but you'll never get there until you start."

Peter Lewis was watching them, his mouth wry. "Women these days are always trying to muscle in on the decision-making," he muttered. "My mother would have got slapped if she had tried to tell my father what to do."

"That sounds like a really happy marriage," Nicola said with a bite. "Just like mine."

There was a silence. Steve looked dangerously at her. Teddy got up, looking at his watch, and said he had to go. The others remembered urgent appointments too, and Steve walked with them to the door.

Joanne gave Nicola a malicious little smile. "That was rather silly of you," she drawled.

"Was it?" Nicola asked coldly.

"There will be repercussions," Joanne said with silky malice. "Mark my words."

"Oh, I will," muttered Nicola, wondering whether to get herself some more whiskey but deciding she just couldn't stand the taste of any more of it.

"Steve's not the sort of guy to take that sort of display in front of his friends." Joanne was looking at her curiously, one hand running through her red hair. Even while they were alone she was never able to forget herself. She posed self-consciously, taking up a catlike attitude of sleek elegance. "I've known him a lot longer than you have."

"Well, that's nice for you," said Nicola, baring her teeth in a smile as false as Joanne's concern.

Joanne gave her another long, considering stare. "You know, I had you down all wrong. I thought you were the domesticated species."

"Oh, did you?" That was what Steve thought too, presumably. He, in common with the rest of his sex, put women into these tidy little categories. It made them easier to cope with and easier to forget.

"No need to bristle at me," Joanne said, looking amused again. "We're on the same side, remember."

I am not on your side, lady, Nicola thought. I'd rather not win than fight alongside you.

"You have to cheat a little," Joanne said. "Kid them along. It doesn't hurt to lie a few times, does it? Let them think they're natural winners if it makes them happy. You should never try a head-on clash. It always ends up with you getting the worst of it."

Nicola looked at her dumbly. Joanne was actually trying to be nice, she saw. Her conspiratorial smile made that clear. It must be fair warning and all that.

"It's called diplomacy," Joanne said. "Try it sometime." She turned her head as Steve came through the door. "I'd better rush," she said, flicking a hand across his cheek in a tantalizing little gesture which Nicola disliked intensely. "See you, darling."

The front door slammed. Steve stood staring at Nicola with furious blue eyes.

Chapter Five

"I ought to slap you," he said, his brown skin drawn tightly over the angular strength of his cheekbones. If she had ever needed to be told that Steve could be dangerous, the way he was staring at her now was an unmistakable reminder.

Nicola was feeling very brave, though. The whiskey was circulating, leaving a comfortable glow inside her, and she looked back at him with her chin lifted belligerently. "Just try it."

"I will, in a minute," he muttered, frowning harshly. "That dress." He gave it a slow appraisal which made her prickle with resentful awareness, his narrowed eyes lingering on the way the bodice clung to her. "It's too tight," he said. "And what do you mean by arguing with me in front of my friends?"

"I didn't argue. I didn't say a word to you."

"Not to me directly," he agreed. "They knew you were sniping at me though—all that stuff about being a free agent."

"That's what you want, though, isn't it? To be free?" She looked coldly at him. "Well, you are. As free as air."

He did not like that. "Don't you ever snarl at my friends again," he said, evading the earlier subject.

"I didn't snarl. I just made myself clear."

"Oh, very clear," he agreed, his face grim. "They've all gone away with the distinct impression that this isn't so much a marriage as a prize fight."

"Well, they're right about one thing. This isn't a marriage. You've never treated me as anything but a woman you sometimes come back to."

His blue eyes took on a glittering threat, his mouth twisting in a bitter smile. "Well, I'm back now," he mocked in a low voice, then crossed the space between them like a streak of lightning.

She looked up, startled, her mouth suddenly dry, the insolent brightness of his gaze sending a shock wave through her body, making her legs go weak underneath her.

"Hello, woman," he taunted in a husky whisper. Her heart distinctly turned over. Nicola had always believed that that was a piece of romantic fantasy. Hearts didn't turn over. Now she discovered that hers did, the strange somersault leaving her quite breathless.

She tried to pull herself together. "Don't you come near me," she hissed aggressively. "We're having a new set of rules around here."

"We certainly are," he agreed, but she didn't get

the impression he was talking about the same set of rules. He was running his eyes over her in that too-tight, sexy dress and taking his time about it. Nicola did not like that look. It made her feel threatened, and, she suspected, that was exactly how he meant her to feel.

"And they're going to be my rules," she said.

"Are you drunk?" he asked, and she lifted an indignant face.

"I only had one glass of whiskey."

"You never could take anything stronger than milk," he taunted, grinning. "Or you wouldn't try to take me on, sweetheart."

"Oh, wouldn't I?"

His arm had somehow insinuated itself around her waist. She looked down at his hand as it calmly appeared beneath the upward swell of her breast.

"Take that away," she demanded. "I don't want it there."

"You're right," he agreed, removing it, then spoiled the effect of this apparent obedience by placing it on her breast, his long fingers splaying to stroke upward.

"Oh," Nicola said with a little gasp.

"It's reprisal time," Steve said silkily, bending to kiss the beating pulse in her throat. His lips were warm and smooth, their sensitive caress sending shivers of pleasure down her spine. She swayed, her eyes closing, and felt his hand shift. The tight bodice of her dress opened and his fingers slipped inside.

"No, no," Nicola said without opening her eyes. She tried to summon up her earlier rage but it seemed to have evaporated. She couldn't remember now what it had all been about. She couldn't remember anything. Her mind submerged beneath waves of pleasure.

The dress had dropped off her shoulders. Without noticing it, she had somehow got her arms around his neck. Under her searching fingers, his thick hair curled and clung. When his mouth closed over hers, she gave a muffled moan of excitement, her lips parting, and Steve drew her closer with one hand while the other softly moved up and down her naked back, following the marked line of her spine.

This wasn't what I meant to happen, Nicola told herself. Then added, more honestly, was it? Under the mounting sexual excitement, her mind was struggling to fight back. There's a principle at stake here, she thought. But what was it?

How could she think with clouds of desire weakening her brain? How could she even hear when her blood was singing in her ears and shutting out every sound but itself? How could she make Steve see her as an equal, a rational human being with a mind of her own, when all he had to do was touch her and she became a puppet, responsive to every movement of his fingers?

Her dress had gone altogether now. She was held against him, his heart beating rapidly, fiercely, against her and his caressing hands growing more urgent as they ran from her breast to her silky thigh.

That's the principle at stake, Nicola remembered suddenly. Here I am again trapped in the same old equation and losing my way as I try to struggle out of it.

Steve saw it as a simple matter. He saw her as the

female to his male, the victim to his victor, and he believed he could always get his equation to add up. All her loud protests could be disregarded so long as Steve knew that he could silence them so easily.

He lifted his head, his eyes half shut, breathing harshly. "I need you, Nicky," he muttered, and her body shook in unwanted, unwilling response.

She wanted him to feel like that. She wanted him to say that. But not until he meant it the way she meant it. Not until Steve understood what needing and wanting meant. At the moment he was still ready to make love to her and walk away afterward, back to the more enthralling world of his job. He had a very limited understanding of love.

"I don't need you," she said, her voice husky and uneven.

The words dropped into silence. Steve's lids lifted. The blue eyes focused on her sharply.

"Liar," he said, trying to smile but visibly taken aback. She had caught him off guard for once. He had been very high and now he had come down with a thud.

"You're sexy, I grant you," she said in a cool voice.

He smiled angrily.

"But then so are lots of men." She smiled back with bland sweetness. "And some of them are rather more reliable."

"Are we back to what's-his-name?" Steve's brows jerked together and an impatient look came into his face. "Don't bring him up again. You know he doesn't turn you on. I could see that. He couldn't turn on a gas fire."

"Martin has nothing to do with this. I'm talking about you. I don't want a husband who comes and goes but usually goes and stays away for months. I want a husband who's around all the time. I want a real marriage, not an intermittent love affair."

Steve's eyes moved restlessly over her, dwelling on the warm white cleft between her breasts under the thin silk slip. "We'll talk about this later, shall we?" He bent and placed his mouth on the smooth exposed flesh. Nicola's breath caught.

"We'll talk about it now," she managed to say hoarsely.

"Darling," he coaxed, sliding his lips over her skin. "There's a more important matter on my mind."

"I know what's on your mind." It was on hers, too, but this time she was not giving in to the tempting persuasion of his kisses. She had to force herself to ignore what he was doing. "I want to talk about the job Teddy Wiseman offered you."

"I'm thinking about it." He gently drew one of the straps of her slip off her shoulder.

Nicola pushed it back up again. "It's just the sort of offer you should accept. You'd get a big raise and you'd be moving up the career ladder several rungs, wouldn't you?"

"Mm," he agreed noncommittally, his finger hooking under her strap to pull it down again.

"Why are you even hesitating?" She slapped his hand. "And stop that."

"I'm not ready to become a vegetable yet," he said, getting irritated, his face faintly red. "Once I leave reporting I'll be stuck at a desk for the rest of my life. You don't go backward in this business. If I take that job, that's it. I'm out of foreign reporting for good."

"You said you planned to leave it one day," she reminded him.

"Not yet," he said in restless impatience. "I'm not interested in sitting at a desk, giving orders, watching other men send in the news. I want to be out there where it's all happening, not standing on the sidelines. It's a different ball game with different rules, Nicky. I need the adrenaline you get from being under fire. If I'd been the sort to sit safely at home, would you have wanted to marry me, anyway?"

"Your job didn't come into my thinking," she said, which was all too painfully true, because she hadn't been doing much thinking. She had been feeling and her mind hadn't been involved at all.

"Do you think you're playing fair?" he asked. "You knew what sort of man I was when you married me. I haven't changed."

"Don't you think perhaps you should have done?" She looked into his eyes and saw them flicker. "You want to have your cake and eat it too, Steve. You want me *and* your old way of life. You want me to make all the adjustments but you don't intend to make any. You said just now that you hadn't changed and that's what's wrong, don't you see? Because one thing *has* changed, Steve. You weren't married, but now you are, and you have to come to terms with that or we might just as well forget about marriage altogether."

"I'm not caving in under ultimatums," he said with sudden savagery. "Married or not, you're not issuing the orders around here."

"It isn't a question of orders. It's more a question of attitude of mind. So long as you continue to think of me as some sort of doll you can pick up and put down at will, I don't want to know about you."

His teeth snapped together. "Right," he said, "So we know where we both stand."

"Yes," Nicola said. "And I'd be grateful if you would get yourself a room at a hotel."

"Right," he said again, in an impeded voice.

"My solicitor tells me that under the new divorce laws I have the right to possession of the marital home."

"Oh, great," Steve said. "You have all the rights and I have none, I gather."

"You must take that up with your solicitor." Nicola could see that he was going to get nasty any minute.

"I ought to take it up with you right now," Steve muttered, giving her a harsh look. "But I'm not going to lose my temper with you. You'd like that, wouldn't you? That's what you've been angling for ever since I got back. Then you'd come into court with some vicious lies about cruelty and ill treatment."

"I don't need lies," Nicola said. "I just have to count up the number of days I've seen you since we were married. That should be enough to convince a court that our marriage never even got off the ground."

"Count away," Steve said. "I didn't know you could count."

"I can do that sum on my fingers," Nicola flung back.

"You can go to hell," he said, striding toward the door. She heard the front door crash open, crash shut. She was trembling, her legs weak under her. She sank down on the couch and sat there blankly for a long time.

She ought to be feeling triumphant. Instead she just felt cold. She had stood fast in defense of her precious principle, but somehow that wasn't much comfort. Principles do not make exciting bedfellows. Nicola wound her arms around herself, biting her lip to stop the tears. If he had been there, he would have had a walk-over at that moment. She told herself she was glad he had gone. It was hard to be convincing, though, when all she could remember was the feel of his hand sliding down her body, the sound of his heart beating next to her own.

What if he goes back to Africa and ends up with a bullet in him? she asked herself, the tears spilling. How will I feel then?

She had taken an enormous risk, gambling that Steve loved her enough to face up to the problem. What if he put his job first? He had before. He very well might again. What then?

Would she be left with nothing but brief, burning memories? It was a bitter prospect, and telling herself that she had been fighting for their future was not going to make it easier.

Nicola had never expected to find herself fighting

so hard for anything. She was not combative by nature; she didn't enjoy quarreling with Steve. It would have been so much easier to let her female instincts rule her and fall into his arms, but she knew that if she had, Steve would have been reinforced in his belief that what he wanted was all that mattered. He would have flown off again when he had a new assignment and Nicola would have been back in the old trap, prey to the old fears and misery.

When she walked into the features department next morning, she was met by a peculiar silence which told her that the excited chatter she had heard as she opened the door had been about her and Steve. Now everyone became very busy, their heads bent over their desks. Nicola pretended she hadn't noticed anything unusual in the atmosphere.

She was not the sort of girl to broadcast her affairs to everyone she met. It was general knowledge, of course, that her marriage to Steve was in trouble; she had not been able to hide that. Her transfer to features had aroused too much curiosity. Most people politely avoided the subject but there was always someone with the tact of an elephant and the curiosity of a jackdaw who seemed oblivious of the fact that his personal questions were unwelcome. Nicola had fenced whenever someone asked a direct question, and her quiet manner had usually managed to silence the questioner.

But that didn't stop the sidelong looks, the unspoken questions, that morning. She worked intently, trying not to notice them.

At lunchtime she did not go down to the canteen.

She went out into a wintry Fleet Street and had a quick salad at a local café. The wind was biting but the sun was trying to fight its way through the clouds blowing across the sky. When she had finished her lunch, Nicola walked down toward St. Paul's to do some hurried shopping. Through the wedge of tower blocks she gazed unseeingly at that stately dome, the sight of it too familiar to penetrate her thoughts.

She was so absorbed that she walked straight into someone, beginning to stammer an apology before she recognized the girl.

"Oh, hello, Jane," she broke off, smiling.

"Wake up," Jane teased, her hazel eyes friendly. She worked in the features department, too, and although they did not know each other very well, they liked each other. Jane was in her early twenties, a shrewd sensible brunette who spent all her spare time ice-skating with her boyfriend.

"I was sleepwalking," Nicola admitted wryly, glancing from Jane to the girl with her. She did not get a very friendly reception there. Mandy Graham had a critical eye. She always spoke her mind, she was fond of explaining, which meant in practice that she was devastatingly rude whenever she felt like it and felt quite justified about it.

"That could be dangerous," Jane said lightly. "Did you eat in the canteen? It could be food poisoning."

Nicola laughed and Jane said, "I'm going back to bringing my own sandwiches. That stew we had today was definitely suspect."

Nicola got the feeling she was talking to stop Mandy coming out with something. Mandy had her eyes fixed unwinkingly on her and she had the expression of someone who was waiting for a chance to speak. Jane began to say something else but Mandy was tired of waiting.

Overriding Jane's voice, she said, "We saw Steve coming out of the lift. Is it true they've offered him the job of Deputy Foreign Editor? Is he going to take it?"

Jane's eyes were ruefully apologetic as Nicola met them. They exchanged glances, then Nicola said calmly, "I don't know. If you ask him, I'm sure he'll tell you."

That was as far as she was prepared to go along the road of giving Mandy back her own coin. Nicola did not like scenes.

Mandy was not amused nor did she even seem to be offended. She had a way of staring at you stolidly, her brown eyes round and bovine, as though trying to force an answer out of you. "Don't you know?" she persisted.

Nicola shook her head, then glanced at her watch. "I must rush. I want to buy some tights." She lifted a hand in a vague wave and hurried away.

Jane caught up with her a few yards further on, falling into step with a sidelong look. "Sorry about her."

"It isn't your fault." Nicola often wondered why Jane put up with Mandy, but office friendships were often more a matter of convenience than personal liking.

"She isn't exactly tactful," Jane said, something hesitant in her manner.

"Not exactly," agreed Nicola. She had a feeling

Jane had more than that to say and was casting around her mind for a way of saying it.

"When something is burning a hole in her head, she just has to let it out," Jane said wryly. She paused. "You ought to know—sooner or later she's going to come out with something else."

"Give it to me," Nicola said lightly, smiling.

"The thing is," Jane muttered, "Steve wasn't alone."

Nicola stopped smiling but her lips curved in a dry, rigid grimace.

"Mandy is going to spill it out to you sometime," Jane said. "She nearly did just now. I thought you'd rather get it from me."

Nicola waited. She wanted to scream at Jane to get it out, not drive her crazy wondering.

"He was with Joanne Hollis," Jane mumbled, rather pink. "Sorry," she added under her breath.

Nicola had five seconds to pull a smile back over her face. She managed it, but it cost her blood. "Oh, that," she said with sparkling vivacity. "I know all about that." She laughed, a silvery little noise which she hoped sounded convincing. "You know Joanne."

Jane stared at her, then looked away. "Who doesn't?"

Nicola stopped to look into a shop window and saw Jane's faintly troubled face beside her own reflection. "I expect they were lunching together," Nicola said. "Joanne wants to move over to foreign and she's hoping to twist Steve's arm."

"Of course," Jane said with false enthusiasm. "That explains it. She's ambitious, isn't she?"

"Very," Nicola muttered.

"Very attractive, of course," Jane said.

"Very," Nicola said again, smiling like mad.

"A bit of a piranha," Jane hesitantly suggested.

"She's all teeth," Nicola said on a bitter rush, then could have kicked herself for betraying so much.

Jane gave a stifled giggle. "I was beginning to wonder if I ought to order your martyr's crown," she said, her eyes dancing.

"Not just yet," Nicola sighed. "Thanks for telling me before anyone else had the chance to take me by surprise with it."

Not that there was much in the news to surprise, she thought, as Jane left her to finish her shopping, but someone less scrupulous than Jane could have got her to betray far more and Nicola would have died if she had let her feelings be seen in public. She would be ready now if someone tried to use the news like some sort of hand grenade.

It was Mandy who did, of course. She sauntered past Nicola that afternoon and halted with a sweetly synthetic smile to say, "Oh, I forgot." Here it comes, thought Nicola, looking happily alert. "Guess who was with Steve," Mandy finished, watching her like a hawk.

"You tell me," Nicola invited.

"Joanne Hollis." Mandy waited with breathless eagerness, staring at her.

"She must be desperate," Nicola said. The phone rang and she answered it, detaching her eyes from Mandy casually. After a moment, Mandy walked away, looking almost shocked.

Across the office Jane signaled "I told you so" and Nicola made a wry little face.

Joe Fraser wandered in an hour later to talk to the features editor. He had a photographer with him who hung around trying to chat up the girls while Joe was closeted with their boss. Mandy liked the brand of repartee which passed for wit with him. She threw it back cheerfully and they laughed a good deal. The other girls were pleased to have an excuse for breaking off work.

The department was housed in an open-plan office full of desks, typewriters, phones and noise. It was used as a through passage from the newsroom to the great bank of steel filing cabinets which held clippings from the back issues of the paper. When Nicola had first started work there, she had found it impossible to ignore the constant comings and goings, but after a while she didn't notice when someone walked through the room. The slap slap of the swinging doors went right over her head. She sometimes felt like a blinkered horse. Head down, she worked, not aware of what was going on around her.

When someone leaned on her desk she looked up, ready to smile. "Oh, hi, Joe."

"How are you?" he asked soberly, as though he hadn't seen her for weeks.

"Fine," she said. She knew he was remembering her little outburst at the party Steve had had in the flat, and she gave him a wry, apologetic smile.

"Raymond says I can borrow you," Joe told her. "I'm doing a feature for him on the circus and he wants it by next week. There's far too much research involved for one person. He says you can go through the files for me. Is that okay with you?"

"I'd enjoy it," she said. It was polite of him to ask since Nicola had no real choice, of course. That was what she was here for—to do what she was told. Joe was always scrupulously courteous, though. "When will you want me to start?"

"Tomorrow," Joe said. "Phil and I are just off to take some shots of a couple of circuses playing around London. Maybe you and I could have a quick session tomorrow at nine? I'll draw up a few guidelines of what I want and let you have a list of names to look up."

"Fine," Nicola said.

The photographer, Phil Smith, came wandering over to give her his insolent smile and a quick inspection which set her teeth on edge. If there was one thing that annoyed her, it was getting that sort of look from men she scarcely knew. She looked back at him with frozen distaste.

"Hello, ice maiden," he said, with another of his smiles.

"Come on," Joe told him grimly.

"You've had your turn," Phil Smith said. "Now I get to chat her up." He winked at Nicola who looked away. "Talk about frost in May," he said. "What's he got that I haven't got?"

"Charm," Nicola said.

Joe chuckled as he dragged the photographer away. Nicola went back to her work, frowning. Over-familiar though Phil Smith always was, he would have drawn the line at that sort of come-on if he hadn't known about the newest blow-up in her marriage. Phil Smith did not try to flirt with married women. He either had some sort of principles or else he did not like trouble.

It was pelting rain as Nicola left the newspaper building that afternoon to make her way home across London. She hesitated under the concrete canopy which overhung the entrance, watching the splash of raindrops into a puddle in the gutter.

A taxi swerved through the busy Fleet Street traffic. Nicola was about to rush across the pavement to hail it when she saw Steve bolt out of the printer's entrance, his hand held up. The taxi pulled in beside him and he opened the door, glancing around. For a second Nicola thought he had seen her and was waiting for her, but even as she was about to join him she saw Joanne Hollis totter across to him on stiltlike heels, her red head bobbing under an umbrella.

Steve took her arm in a chivalrous gesture to slide her into the cab, then he shut the umbrella and got in beside her. The taxi chugged away, engine throbbing as it waited for a break in the line of cars. Nicola stared fixedly at the two heads she could see in the rear window. Steve was leaning toward Joanne, his bronzed profile clearly visible. Joanne put up a hand to brush back a rain-soaked lock of black hair from his forehead, then she ran her fingertips lightly down his jaw.

Nicola was swamped by a wave of jealous hatred which left her feeling sick.

She was not surpirsed, of course. She had known as she watched Joanne with Steve at the flat that the other woman fancied him and Steve had not exactly been slapping her down. The shrouded secrets of Steve's past love life could contain any number of other women, but Nicola knew nothing about them. The faceless procession she had always imagined had been a hidden threat to her peace of mind and she could not decide whether it was harder or easier to be able to put a face to what she had long suspected.

Steve's sexuality was too vital for her to imagine he had led a blameless life before he met her, but that had not mattered too much beside the realization that his affairs had never meant much to him. Looked at in a certain light that might seem reassuring. Steve had married her because he loved her, she had tried to tell herself. He had never loved any of the others.

Nicola had never been able to convince herself. The attitude of contempt and indifference which underlay Steve's casual treatment of women had been a dark thread in their relationship, too. It was the reason why he had married her and then rushed back to his job. Steve despised the opposite sex. He had always been able to get any woman he wanted. Nicola had tumbled at his feet the minute he looked in her direction. He expected it.

But not anymore, Steve, she thought. I'd rather lose you than spend the rest of my life as the wallpaper hanging in the ignored background of your life.

Chapter Six

Great newspapers always carry a vast filing system from which reporters can dig out background facts to enrich the mixture of their stories. Nicola was used to quarrying in the Morgue, as it was known. All the back copies of the paper were stored there, along with everything known about anyone whose name had appeared in the paper in the past.

The huge room was always crowded with people rushing from one cabinet to the other in search of information. The staff had a calm, phlegmatic patience. You couldn't hurry them. They picked their way through the files carefully and could reel off the correct catalogue numbers on almost any subject. They had a row of shelves behind their desks which held reference books to back up what the files contained. The more esoteric a subject the more they enjoyed the challenge of finding out about it.

Nicola spent most of the following day in there, making elaborate notes in shorthand in a large notebook. She found it fascinating to read the history of the modern circus. Joe was spending the day looking for still photographs to go with his feature. Wryly, he had said that that would be the hardest part of the whole job. He already knew he could only have two pictures with his article and he was going to have to choose from a rich array of fantastic shots.

The cabinets were arranged in narrow alleys along which you had to squeeze if you wanted to pass someone else who was consulting one of the steel drawers. Nicola stood, flicking over files, with people occasionally apologizing behind her as they passed and forced her to move.

"Fancy meeting you here," a voice suddenly murmured intimately in her ear and she looked around in startled surprise.

"Oh," she murmured, her lips parting, color sweeping up her face. Today he looked quite different, far more rested, the strain and weariness she had seen in his face when he first got back quite gone. Steve was tough. He recovered quickly.

"What are you up to?" he asked, glancing at her notebook and then at the files she was consulting.

"Researching." Her eyes quickly flicked over him while he was not aware of it. He was wearing a new suit, she noticed. It was more formal than the clothes he usually bought. Steve wore jeans more often than suits, his taste casual.

Was he going somewhere special? The suit looked very good on him, the dark jacket open to show a close-fitting waistcoat which emphasized his slim waist and his crisp white shirt showing up that smooth, tanned skin.

"Researching what?" he asked, looking at her before she could look away.

Her color deepening, she muttered, "Joe's doing a feature on the circus."

"There's an apt subject," Steve said. "Joe should know all about clowns." He grinned, though. She knew he liked Joe.

Nicola detached her eyes from their survey of his lean-hipped figure. "Have you been to see Margaret yet?"

Steve had a casual attitude to family relationships. His sister, Margaret, saw little of him. Steve rarely visited her and even more rarely wrote. She had said, last time Nicola saw her, that it was only the occasional postcard that told her Steve was alive.

"Not yet." Impatience showed in the way his mouth tightened. "All I would get is a string of questions. Maggie never could mind her own business."

"She's very fond of you."

He made a face. "She's very fond of trying to boss me around, you mean."

"If you're only intending to stay in England for a few days, you ought to make the effort to drive over to Suffolk."

His dark lashes drooped suddenly across his brown cheek. "Don't nag," he said, watching her through them. "What's it to you? I thought you had washed your hands of me."

"I'm fond of Margaret."

His eyes mocked her. He knew Margaret made her feel hunted, too. "Come with me, then," he said, grinning.

I walked right into that, Nicola told herself. She shook her head firmly. "No, thank you. She's your sister, not mine."

"I thought you said you liked Margaret," he said innocently.

She didn't answer, her eyes sarcastic. He knew why she did not want to accompany him, and it had nothing to do with liking or disliking his sister.

Margaret was a lively woman in her late thirties with dark hair and blue eyes like her brother's, a slim active figure and enough energy for six women. She lived in a small village in Suffolk near the edge of some rough marshland. Margaret ran that village. She had three children and a busy doctor for a husband yet she found time to preserve her own fruit and jams, make her own bread, do all her own housework and still dictate the social life of every other woman in the village. Any social function organized there was capably masterminded by Margaret. Any local society only functioned under her eagle eye. She made Nicola feel weak and inadequate.

Steve had never hidden his view that Margaret was only to be taken in small doses. When he was young, his sister had organized his life, too, and he had been relieved to escape from her sharp-eyed dictatorship.

"I'm not going down there alone," he said, wistfully, now.

"Take Joanne Hollis," Nicola snapped, her color rising.

His eyes narrowed and a satisfied little smile curved his lips. "What a good idea," he said softly.

Nicola looked back at the files, her fingers tightening on the steel edge of the drawer. Why don't I keep my mouth shut? she asked herself.

"Very fetching creature, Joanne," he drawled, watching her with acute observation.

"I've seen her doing the fetching," Nicola said. "She's like a good gundog. She doesn't ruffle a feather on their backs."

"Meow," Steve mocked. "Now what gives me the idea you don't like her?"

"I don't give her a thought," Nicola lied.

"No?" He looked smug as her eyes flicked at him and away. She would have loved to wipe that satisfaction off his face.

"No," she said, slamming the drawer and almost catching her hand in it in her haste.

Steve saw her jerk of alarm and asked, "Hurt yourself?" He took her wrist before she could back off and viewed her hand for signs of injury. Her small pale fingers looked very colorless against the brown strength of his and Steve turned her hand palm upward, touching the center of her palm with one long finger.

"Tiny little hands," he said huskily. "You should be more careful. That skin of yours shows every mark."

Her breathing quickened. He lifted her hand to

his mouth, brushing his lips gently on the palm. Someone came hurrying around the end of the cabinets and Steve released her, faint color in his face.

Nicola walked away, her eyes down, trying to halt the queer trembling in the pit of her stomach. She went over to the desk to consult the clerk and a few moments later she saw Steve leaving.

At five o'clock Joe came into the features department and Nicola paused in her typing. "Hi," he said in his flat voice. A stocky, quiet man in his thirties, Joe was already slightly balding, his hair receding at great speed from the high dome of his forehead. Peering at the page in her typewriter, he asked, "How's it going?"

"I got all the checking done," she told him. "I'm just typing up my notes for you now."

"Oh, great. Can you let me have it tonight before you go?"

She looked at the clock and at once Joe added, "If it isn't any trouble." He was much easier to work with than some of the reporters. They had more sense of urgency and more sense of their own importance. Nicola had worked for Steve, and she knew he was the worst offender where that sort of attitude was concerned. Steve knew he was the hub and purpose of the universe. The world, in his opinion, revolved around him and he expected any work you did for him to be ready when he wanted it. Steve had no notion of other people's convenience or any sense of time. That was what made him such a good reporter. It didn't make him easy to work for.

"I'll try," Nicola promised and got one of Joe's calm, friendly smiles.

"Thanks." He did not waste words. "Bring it through to me when you're ready," he said. "I'll be at my desk."

At six she still hadn't quite finished but the other girls had gone, sheathing their typewriters and drifting out, talking. The great room had an empty feel under the blaze of the strip lighting. People still came and went through the swinging doors, their feet tapping along past her, but Nicola did not look up, her eye fixed on the notes she was transcribing.

It was almost seven when she finally finished the last line. She sat back, eyes closed, very tired. Her back was aching and her eyes were weary from staring at the squiggly shorthand.

"You look terrible."

She opened her eyes and gave Joe a wry smile. "Thanks, that's very comforting."

He was eyeing her with compunction. "If I'd realized it was going to take you so long, I wouldn't have asked you to finish it tonight. It could have waited until morning."

"Now he tells me," she said, grinning.

"I'm sorry," Joe apologized.

"It was no trouble," she said. She collected up the pages and clipped them together, handing them over with another smile. "There you are—would you like to check them now?"

"That can wait," he said. "You shoot off home, Nicola. Thank you very much for all the work."

He walked out of the room with her and on the stone-floored landing, as they both waited for the lift down to the ground floor, they talked politely about the notes. "I enjoyed reading it all," Nicola assured him. "I was fascinated. I love the circus. I always used to enjoy going although I didn't care much for the animal acts, particularly the big cats. I think that's rather cruel. I can't believe it can be done with kindness, that sort of training. It's too unnatural."

Joe nodded soberly. "I think people only enjoy those acts because they half hope to see the trainer getting his head bitten off."

The lift stopped and they were met with cries of "No room, no room" from the crush of people inside it. Joe grimaced, moving back, and the doors closed again. There was always a long wait for lifts at this hour of the evening. The paper was reaching the peak period of activity before the deadline arrived.

"It might be quicker to use the stairs," Joe told her.

Nicola grinned. "I'm too tired. But you can if you're in a hurry, Joe. Don't let me keep you."

"I'm not in a hurry," he said, eyeing her with unhidden concern. "You do look tired. Your skin is always pale but tonight you look gray."

"That's what I like to hear," Nicola said lightly. "All this flattery will go to my head."

They heard the click of footsteps behind them. Nicola half turned and saw Joanne Hollis walking out of the newsroom with Steve at her heels. Joanne was talking in her light, quick voice and giving Steve one of her eyelash-fluttering smiles.

"It came over on the telex," she said. "An hour ago—another one of those quakes."

"Not my scene," Steve said, his blue eyes narrowed as he halted next to Nicola. "Well, well," he drawled. "If it isn't my wife."

Joanne laughed. Nicola ground her teeth, averting her eyes. The lift stopped, the doors slid open and Nicola walked into it with the others following her. She would rather die than allow herself to show a thing.

Joanne turned to view herself in the mirror on the wall of the lift, running a satisfied hand over her flaming hair, adjusting the tight belt of her green dress. "Going out for a supper break, Joe?" she asked as she turned around again.

He gave her a nod. "You?" He wasn't looking at Steve but Nicola was, her angry eyes watching him from behind lowered lashes. Steve was looking at Joanne with a lazy smile, but as if he felt Nicola's stare, he flickered a glance at her, taunting mockery in his blue eyes.

"We're having dinner at Ramiro's," Joanne purred, putting a hand on Steve's arm, her polished nails gleaming against the dark material of his jacket.

Nicola's hands clenched at her sides, the nails digging into her soft palms. She lifted her head, staring at the lift doors as it descended. She could feel them all looking at her. Joanne was smiling like a cat that has stolen the cream. She was competitive, feline, a woman whose nature it is to covet other women's property. Nicola fought not to show the bitter jealousy which was consuming her, biting into her inner lip to keep her mouth steady.

Calmly, Joe said, "Nicky and I are eating out, too, but I can't afford Ramiro's on my salary. All I can manage is the local Indian place—Chicken Madras for me, I like a nice curry." He grinned at Steve slightly. "I don't get my dinners on expenses, like some."

The lift stopped and Nicola walked out blindly. "Hang on, wait for me, Nicky," Joe said, hurrying after her, leaving Steve and Joanne to follow at a slower pace. Nicky waited, trembling, and together they walked out into the dark night. Fleet Street was a different place at this hour, all the traffic slowing to a trickle, the pavements empty except for a few printers here and there, talking and smoking.

Joe caught her elbow and steered her across the road. "I hope you didn't mind," he said.

"No," Nicola muttered, giving him a shaky little smile. "Thanks, Joe."

He flushed. The night wind lifted the thinning locks of his hair and blew them forward over the bald patch. "Joanne can be a bit much," he said.

"Just the tiniest bit," Nicola said tartly.

He laughed. "I suppose you wouldn't agree to eating a curry with me? It isn't bad at Mohal's. He does all the cooking himself and it's always edible."

"I've eaten there," she said. "I like their curry and I'd love to have a Chicken Madras with you, Joe."

"That's fine," he said, walking down the tiny side road which ended in the Thames embankment. Below them lay the dark waters of the river, their oily surface glinting with reflected yellow light. The sky behind the Thames was jagged with tower blocks, windows lit in some cases, in others pitch dark now that the office staff had gone.

"I like London at night," Nicola murmured.

"I like it any time," Joe told her, his face wry. "I was brought up in a small town in Cheshire. Come six o'clock and the place shut down for the night. I much prefer London."

They had reached the Indian restaurant whose oriental lamps glowed in the night like strange fruit. Joe shepherded her to a table and they ordered. They were the only customers. At lunchtime though, the place was always crowded. Office workers liked the lunchtime menu which was a set price meal with coffee thrown in, the price temptingly reasonable. "I've only eaten here at lunchtime," Nicola said. "It seems different at night." The heavy red curtains were drawn and the room had a hushed intimacy quite unlike the busy rush earlier in the day.

Joe had little to say and it was hard work making conversation with him. She was grateful to him for the way he had charged in to rescue her, but that did not help her to keep up a flow of small talk.

He relaxed more while they were eating, as though having the food on the table made it easier for him to be natural with her. Offering her a *paratha,* he said, "It must have been tough for you, with Steve away so much."

"Yes," she said, refusing the *paratha* with a smile. There was far too much food. "Why do they bring so much?" she asked Joe. "They must think we've got huge appetites."

He nodded, but he was determined to discuss Steve. "He isn't an easy guy," he said. "The way he's always lived demands a very self-sufficient sort of mind."

Nicola looked at the curry. She wished he would stop talking about Steve. It was ruining her appetite. "Self-sufficient describes him perfectly," she said.

"But nobody is," Joe said. "Not entirely self-sufficient."

She pushed her curry around the plate with a fork. It was very well cooked but she just did not want it. "Steve comes pretty close," she sighed.

"He took that business in Africa hard," Joe muttered. "I've never seen him so shaken by anything. He only just got out of there alive, did he tell you? One of the government troops hid him. Steve knew him, you see. They'd been out drinking together."

How typical, thought Nicola. They had a few drinks together and that made them pals. Men make me sick.

"I don't want to talk about it," she said. Her stomach was heaving. If Steve wanted to walk along a cliff edge, she couldn't stop him but she did not want to hear about it.

"He doesn't show what he's feeling most of the time," Joe said. "But seeing all those killings . . ."

"Don't," Nicola bit out. Reading about it had been bad enough. She did not want to talk about it.

"He's human," Joe insisted. "I know how he feels. He's angry, sick, horrified. And he's feeling guilty, too."

"Guilty about what?" She stared at him, bewildered.

"Being alive," Joe said flatly. "You know what he said to me? 'Why me?' he said. 'Why did I get out alive?' "

Nicola's lip trembled. "Maybe next time he won't," she said with savage pain, and Joe fell silent for a long time, as though recognizing he had said enough. It was some time before he spoke again.

"Joanne is a troublemaker," he said. "It isn't wise to give her the room to make trouble."

"She can only make as much trouble as Steve allows," Nicola said resentfully.

"Nature abhors a vacuum," Joe told her. "Didn't you learn that at school?"

"What if the vacuum existed anyway?" She did not look up to meet his eyes.

There was a little silence. The waiter brought the bill and Joe paid it before guiding her out of the restaurant. He insisted on putting her into a taxi and the subject of Steve did not come up again.

It was hard to go back to her silent flat, knowing that Steve was in the same city, but with another woman, and her imagination was working overtime as she sat listening to the ticking of the clock and the beat of the rain against the window.

It was not the first time, though, that she had sat here wondering jealously what he was doing, and at least her angry emotion was not increased by the fear that he was in deadly danger, risking his life for the sheer thrill of it. That had been unbearable.

When she got to the office next morning, Jane came over to groan about delays on the underground. "It took me an hour to get here today. In theory it's supposed to take twenty-five minutes. Staff shortages, they said. Living in London is becoming a nightmare."

"I came by bus," Nicola said. "That took ages,

too. I'm beginning to think it would be quicker to walk."

"You and me both," Jane grimaced.

Mandy walked toward them, and with a blank face Nicola hurriedly moved away. She wasn't letting herself in for any more of Mandy's prying comments about Steve.

The grapevine would already be busy with rumors about him and Joanne. She knew how people around here talked, but she wasn't listening to any of it. Her imagination could work hard enough without any help from the grapevine.

It wasn't easy to stop people talking to her, though. They took such devious routes to bring the subject up. All day she kept getting oblique comments and all day she kept changing to some other topic. Of course, they all wanted to know how she felt about Steve seeing Joanne. Nicola refused to give anything away.

She went home dead on time that evening. As soon as she let herself into the flat she knew Steve was there. She could hear him whistling under his breath in the kitchen.

A tide of rage swelled up inside her. She flung open the door and he looked drily at her furious face.

"I thought I told you . . ."

"I came to collect some things," he broke in before she had finished. "I went in such a hurry that I left behind a pile of papers I shall need."

"You should have asked me for them, not just walked in here." He was wearing jeans again, with a thick white fisherman's jersey, and he looked tougher than ever. Just the sight of him made her feel nervous.

He folded his arms, surveying her closely. "Did Joe stand you a good dinner?"

She met his stare with an assumed smile. "Yes, thank you. I enjoyed the evening very much. Joe's a nice man."

He gave her a jeering little smile. "Of course he is—just up your street. Joe's out of the same box as the stockbroker guy, isn't he? Another tame, security-minded type who will never be any problem to you. That's what you want to turn me into, isn't it? A nine-to-five commuter who trots home to you to get his head patted and his dinner put in front of him. You don't want a man—you want a dog."

"That's not true," she said angrily. "You're twisting things around again. You refuse to face facts."

"It's you who's doing that. *I'm* a fact. Myself, the way I am—that's a fact. I'm not the nine-to-five type."

"You mean you're not husband material! Well, okay, shove off then," she said with burning bitterness. "Who asked you to come here to shout at me? I'm giving you a divorce. You'll be free. Clear off and be yourself somewhere else."

"Maybe I will," he said, his temper rising too. "There are other women in the world and I don't get complaints from them."

"Joanne Hollis," she interpreted, her amber eyes hardening.

"Joanne," he mocked, his mouth twisting. "She's

a realist. She doesn't expect me to be anything but what I am."

"I'm sure she doesn't. She's just your type, if we're going to start classifying people. Joanne Hollis plays the field too."

His icy glare made her smile in angry sarcasm. He threw back, "I do not play the field, blast you."

"And you never have, of course," she said, hating him.

He shifted, shrugging his wide shoulders. "If you're talking about before I met you, well, maybe a little. Don't we all before we settle for someone?"

"You didn't settle for me. You just married me. There was no settling involved. Joanne is welcome to you. She should suit you nicely—I get the feeling she likes it without strings, too."

"She always has," he grated, cynical amusement in his blue eyes suddenly.

They looked at each other in taut silence. "I always suspected you had known her very well in the past," Nicola said.

His eyes flickered. He didn't answer but she knew him too well; he didn't need to. "Yes," she said. She was right; he and Joanne had known each other intimately some time. Joanne had hinted as much to her.

"Well, at least she knows what she's getting," Nicola muttered. "I had to find out the hard way."

"She isn't getting anything," he said with growing impatience.

"Not yet? Don't keep her waiting too long." Nicola was using a tone of voice she had never used in her life before, but then, she had never been so angry before, either. It was acting on her like acid. Her voice sounded raw and sharp. I sound hateful and vicious, she thought incredulously, but she couldn't stop herself.

"Nicky," he said hoarsely, staring at her. "Don't talk like that."

"Maybe I should take a leaf out of her book. Obviously I don't know what I've been missing. All this freedom is going to the wrong people. Why shouldn't I take advantage of it too?"

"Don't be ridiculous," he muttered, his frown black.

"You ought to approve," she said. "You can't expect to be set free without leaving me free, too. I'll have to start finding out what fun it is to have no ties."

He crossed the room in two strides and shook her violently, rage in his face. "I'm not listening to any more of it."

"You don't have to listen. There's the door. Go through it and don't come back." She was past being alarmed by his height or the dominating power of his blue eyes. She looked back at his angry face, defiant. "And give me back my key, too. I don't want you using this flat whenever you feel like it. I have no intention of coming back one evening to find you and Joanne in my bedroom."

His hands bit into her shoulders. "You little . . ."

She struggled, shoving at him to escape, but her slight build gave her no chance against his strength and Steve shook her again, her head swinging from side to side, the strands of dark hair whipping across her face.

"Let me go," she raged.

He stopped shaking her, staring down at her in grim silence. "No," he said thickly.

Suddenly Nicola was frightened. Her heart gave a convulsive leap. She stared up at him, unable to drag her eyes away from the dark intention she could see in his eyes. Swallowing, she said in a shaking little voice, "Don't."

"I'm going to," he said in that deep, hoarse voice, and her fear grew like a fire fed with petrol.

Under her fear a weak, smoldering excitement began to grow, too. "I should have done this the night I got back," Steve said, then he picked her up like a child, heaving her over his shoulder.

"Put me down," she gasped, banging on his broad shoulders with her fists, kicking her legs vainly, her head dizzy as he began to walk toward the bedroom. "You dare!" she screamed. "Steve, I'll never forgive you. You can't. I don't want to . . ."

"I don't care two cents what you want."

He kicked open the bedroom door, the wood crashing as the door hit the wall behind it. The next second Nicola was flung down on the bed, her helpless body off balance as she looked up at him, her eyes wide and nervous.

He flung his sweater to the floor, his bare brown chest gleaming in the light streaming in from the living room. As he began to take off his jeans Nicola tried to struggle off the bed on the other side. He grabbed her roughly and forced her back, his deep, hurried breathing sounding very loud in the room.

"You're my wife," Steve roared at her. "It's time you got that through your head."

"It isn't me who needs to realize that," Nicola told him in a bitter voice. "You say I'm your wife—you don't claim to be my husband."

"Don't let's start that again," he grated.

"It works both ways. You want me as your wife but you have no intention of behaving like a husband."

"The devil I haven't," he muttered. "I'm going to behave like one right now."

His lean body forced her back against the pillows, his mouth hungrily closing over hers, a fierce compulsive demand in the movement of it as it parted her lips. Nicola fought against her own weak need to yield to him. When she struggled, his hands and mouth grew almost brutal, refusing to allow her to escape. Under his passion his anger still raged, the savage insistence with which he made her give way to him a betrayal of it.

Her struggles weakened and as they did so her own desire flared up to meet his. Moaning, she relaxed under him, her hands grasping his black hair.

Feeling that surrender, his hands began to stroke down her body and she felt her bones turning to wax inside her overheated flesh. She had been wanting to touch him for days. Ever since she saw him in her bed her body had been aching for this, and with trembling hands she touched his throat, his shoulders, the muscled chest, her skin burning at the feel of his flesh against it.

Her dress slid down and his exploring hands began to peel off her slip, his head buried between her breasts, blazing a path down her body which brought a weak moan from her. They had always been passionate lovers, but there had never been this stark necessity between them before. Steve lifted his head as he heard the cry she gave and his face held a confused mixture of triumph, hunger, desire. He was breathing as fast as she was, his skin burning hot.

"Darling," he whispered. "I need to make love to you. You need it, too, don't you?"

The weak, feminine side of her nature cried out in yielding agreement. Nicola's brain struggled to drown that cry. During her months alone while Steve was in Africa other elements had been working in her like leaven, changing her whole attitude. If I give in now, I give in forever, she recognized. It wasn't love. It was war. Steve meant to win that war. He might not even know what he was doing; he acted instinctively. Faced with her rebellion against his wishes he was falling back on the male imperative.

They had each retreated to entrenched positions—sniping at each other from opposite sides of the no-man's land between them. They were in a hand-to-hand, body-to-body struggle now, and in that conflict Nicola had little hope of winning. Steve had all the advantages. The driving, urgent power of his body could always defeat her. How could he lose with her instincts fighting on his side? The woman in her craved surrender, primitive instincts from a buried racial memory confident that that was the female way to win.

It had always worked for women in the past. When they softly submitted to the possessing male, they engulfed him with their warm bodies, possessing him in the act of possession, retaining him when he withdrew, always the victors on the abandoned field of battle which the man imagined he had conquered. Women had weapons too subtle and too secret to defeat. Waxing and waning like the moon, they drew men like the tides, men helpless in their own strength, blind to their captivity.

Nicola was fighting a different war, though. Steve was a nomad, always wandering away from her, and she could not fight that with a gentle surrender. It had not held him in the past. She had no hope it would hold him now.

He was kissing her fiercely, her head framed in his hands, but his urgency was growing. He moved away to strip off the rest of his clothes. Nicola slid off the bed, taking the quilt with her. She folded herself into it and Steve turned, lifting his head in surprise.

He was smiling, though. The hard planes of his naked body had a taut excitement as he moved toward her, laughing under his breath. "Give up, darling. You know you're going to."

"I can't stop you," she admitted stiffly. "But if you do—I'll never forgive you."

"Don't be stupid, Nicky," he said, still amused.

'I mean it. Steve! I mean it!" The last words were yelled, their sound clear and bitter.

He stopped dead in his tracks, a hand's breadth away. The blue eyes focused on her searchingly; his frown deepened.

"You wanted it just now; don't lie," he said undeniably.

"All right, I did," she admitted, deciding that there was no point in lying to him. "And I want it now," she went on, throwing that out huskily. She saw his frown vanish and his smile come back. The blue eyes held amused mockery.

"Darling," he said, about to touch her again.

"But I *won't,*" she said fiercely, through her teeth. "Do you hear me, Steve? I *won't.*"

His frown returned, darker than ever. "I should think half the street could hear you," he muttered. "Don't shout like that."

"It seems I have to shout to make you listen," she said. "I don't enjoy shouting. It makes my head ache."

"It makes mine ache, too" he said harshly, staring at her. "You've given me a permanent headache since I arrived back."

"Try using your head then," Nicola advised. "It's simple enough. I want a marriage based on respect, if you like."

"So do I," he retorted.

She shook her head. "No, Steve. You demand my respect but you don't give me any. If you can't bear living in London, take me with you. I don't mind where I live so long as I'm with you but I'm sick of living alone and I'm sick of this pretense of a marriage. Make up your mind about it. If you want me as your wife, you have got to change the way we've been living. Until you're ready to do that, you're not sleeping with me."

His eyes were metallic blue slits under the black line of his brows. She met them without any visible sign of alarm, her soft mouth hardening in determination. Nicola was fighting for her life, her back was to the wall, and she had no intention of backing down. Steve saw it. He swore savagely under his breath, the word too muffled to be audible, then he whirled in a movement jerky with temper, and snatched up his clothes. She watched, huddled in the quilt like a defiant squaw, while he dragged them on in rough haste.

When he was dressed he turned on her, his eyes shooting at her like bullets. "I was all wrong about you, wasn't I?" At last he was getting the message. "You're not the woman I took you for."

Nicola was glad he had noticed, her eyes told him.

"I thought you were so gentle," he accused in response to that look. There is a time and place for gentleness but the battlefield is not it, she thought.

"I thought you were just the woman I'd been looking for all my life." She could believe that. Steve wanted a woman who would never make any demands on him, who would yield and accept without question. She gave him a sarcastic little smile which brought a flare of red into his face.

"You're about as gentle as a bulldozer," he said viciously. "I don't admire women who lay down the law." Of course he didn't. If anyone was going to lay down laws, it was going to be he. That was how he saw the role of the male.

"I'm not running my life to please you," Steve grated. He ran his life to please himself and he expected his wife to fall in with it, no matter what it cost her. The world was masculine territory, run by men, organized by them, their birthright from the moment they opened their eyes. The female role was to accept, submit, do as she was told.

Nicola had tacitly understood that. It would never

have entered her head to challenge her sexual role if Steve had not placed the strain of fear and anguish on their marriage. He might not realize it but she was fighting for him as much as for herself. She wasn't humbly sitting at home while he risked his life for the kick he got out of it.

"Why don't you say something?" he demanded, glaring at her.

"I've said all I had to say."

"You obstinate little fool!" Steve roared, then he turned and stalked to the door. "Maybe Joanne will be more welcoming," he threatened as he opened it, and she knew he was waiting for her to call him back, his body poised in the doorway.

"Don't forget, I want the key to my flat," she said, unmoved.

The slam of the door almost deafened her. She trembled in the folds of the quilt. The strain of their fighting was eating at her nerves. Tears spilled from her eyes. Now that he had gone she stumbled to the bed and lay there, weeping for a long time.

Chapter Seven

During the rest of that week Nicola was in a state of numbed suspension. She hardly knew what she was doing at work. She got through each day without anything that happened remaining in her head. People spoke to her and she answered them, but when they went away she could not have told anyone what they had said.

"Are you okay?" Jane asked, and Nicola looked at her blankly, a polite smile on her mouth.

"Sure."

"Sure?" Jane did not look convinced. "You're sleepwalking again, aren't you?" she teased with so much sympathy in her hazel eyes that Nicola wanted to cry, but she smiled again somehow.

"Am I? Sorry."

Jane had the hesitant look which meant she felt

she ought to say something but wasn't quite sure how to phrase it or whether it would be wiser not to say it at all.

"Steve's been having some long sessions with Teddy Wiseman, hasn't he?"

"Has he?" Nicola shrugged. "Debriefing sessions, I expect. He's probably giving his successor a rundown on the situation over there, the civil war."

Jane looked at her sharply. "Oh, is that what's going on?"

"I expect so."

"Steve isn't going to take the Deputy Editor job, then?"

"You, too?" Nicola asked with a dry glance and Jane went rather pink, making a little face.

"Sorry, I was prying, wasn't I?"

"The tiniest bit," Nicola agreed, her face breaking into a smile at the other girl's self-accusing tone.

"I ought to know better, but everyone keeps speculating about it. Rumor is rife."

Rumor ran around the newspaper offices at lightning speed. It reminded Nicola of the dome of St. Paul's—whisper something at one side and it is heard right around the other side a second later, and not always accurately. What people did not know, they guessed or invented.

"They *are* all dying to know what Steve will do," Jane said.

"They'll have to wait and see, won't they?" Nicola had no intention of admitting to Jane that she was waiting, too. Jane no doubt imagined that Steve had discussed it with her. Nicola had gambled and now she was waiting for the spin of the wheel which would tell her whether she had won or lost. Her need to know was much greater than that of the other staff members. Her whole future depended on it.

Joanne wandered past Nicola's desk that afternoon and paused to give her that sweetly feline smile. "Hi," she said, skating an assessing look over Nicola's face. "How are you?"

"Fine, how are you?" Nicola wondered what had brought Joanne in here and did not believe it was chance. Joanne was here with a purpose.

Joanne leaned on her desk, the curve of her body lazy. "I just heard a new rumor," she murmured.

"Oh?" Nicola watched her, a line between her brows.

"A little bird told me you and Steve were getting a divorce. Is that so?"

Nicola stiffened. "Ask him," she said, her whole body tense with anger.

Joanne's moist red mouth curled in a mocking smile. "I don't need to, do I? If it wasn't true, you'd have denied it."

Nicola began to type violently. "I'm busy," she said. "Do you mind?"

Joanne laughed and clicked away on her high heels, her body swaying with exaggerated sex appeal. Nicola threw a look after her. She wished it had been a knife.

Steve strode through the room an hour later. He did not stop nor did he look in her direction, slamming through into the Morgue without seeming to be aware of her presence. Mandy drifted over afterward to say, "Is it true that Joanne Hollis is going out to do a tour of the Middle East?"

Nicola looked up. "Where did you hear that?"

"Someone was talking about it in the canteen—Joanne has been angling for a job on foreign for months. It seems she finally got what she wanted."

Nicola pretended indifference and Mandy reluctantly went away. As she worked, Nicola wondered if it was true. It would remove Joanne from dangerous contact with Steve. When Joe came by and stopped to chat about his article, she waited for a chance to ask him about it.

It was hard to pretend an interest she did not genuinely feel. All her attention was centered on Steve, her mind drivingly obsessed with the need to know what he was doing.

Joe broke off to peer at her, frowning. "I'm boring you."

"No," she said quickly, smiling. "I'm fascinated by the circus."

"But you're on edge about Steve," he said shrewdly, and she laughed, her face wry.

"Sorry, does it show that much?"

"Neither of you shows much," Joe said. "In your different ways you're both pretty secretive, aren't you?"

"Are we?" Nicola hadn't thought she was but what does one ever know of oneself? From inside a life it's impossible to guess how it looks from the outside. Everyone's viewpoint is fixed at an angle dictated by a very subjective attitude. We only see life from our own pair of eyes. Maybe it would be easier, she thought, if we could occasionally switch heads and see how it looks from another angle, but life isn't arranged like that.

"You aren't exactly a chatterbox," Joe teased.

"No," she agreed. She found it so hard to make conversation. "I'm sorry."

"You're shy," Joe said. "And I wish you wouldn't keep apologizing for yourself." There was a touch of irritation in the way he said that and she flushed.

"Do I? Sorry." Then she laughed.

"You see? There you go again. You say that word far too often. Why should you apologize for being yourself? I like your quiet company." He was slightly flushed, his eye sliding away from her.

Nicola flushed too. It hadn't occurred to her before but now she hoped Joe was not taking too much interest in her. She liked him, but only as a friend.

"Some people are hard to talk to," Joe said. "Joanne Hollis, for instance—she makes me feel stupid. She talks too easily. Every man she meets gets some sort of come-on and you know she doesn't mean a word of it. It's all show. She makes me want to run a mile away from her."

Nicola waited until he had stopped talking before asking him, "I'd heard she was going out to the Middle East soon?"

She was surprised when Joe shot her a strange look, his forehead creasing in a frown. "I wouldn't know," he said, but his eyes moved away far too quickly. He looked at his watch. "Good heavens, look at the time, I must rush." He was gone like a rabbit disappearing down a rabbithole and Nicola stared after him in anxious speculation.

Over the next two days she saw Steve only at a distance. Martin rang her one evening but she refused his invitation to have dinner that night. "You aren't changing your mind about the divorce?" he asked her, and she sighed, and said she had not altered her plans. She didn't tell him that her plans depended entirely upon Steve's decision.

"Martin, I like you, but I'm not in love with you, you know," she said uncertainly. "I don't think you're in love with me, either, if you're honest with yourself."

"We hadn't got that far," he said in an offended voice. "Had we? I'd hardly been allowed to kiss you."

He rang off sulkily and Nicola sighed. Martin was a complication in an already complicated situation. She could have done without his intervention to-night. Although she knew he did not love her, she felt guilty about dating him in the first place. She had known in the back of her mind that she didn't really fancy him at all. He had been an antidote to Steve, that was all, his calm quiet manner soothing to her when she was deeply unhappy.

She had lunch with Joe the next day. It hadn't been planned; they just happened to arrive in the canteen at the same time and queued up together, talking about a freak hailstorm which had smashed some windows on the other side of London.

Nicola wasn't unaware of the whisper of comment following them as they sat down at a spare table. Her cheeks rather pink, she avoided Joe's eyes, wishing they had not bumped into each other at the door.

"Enjoying yourselves?" They both looked up as Joanne purred at them. She was alone, but Nicola did not need three guesses to know that Joanne would make sure Steve heard about his wife lunching with his best friend. Joanne had the glint in her eyes of someone suddenly given a birthday present. She did not wait for an answer, swaying away with a broad smile.

Joe looked at Nicola wryly. "Sorry, dumb of me not to realize it would cause talk."

"I don't care," Nicola muttered untruthfully. She felt the eyes staring from all sides and she couldn't wait to get this week finished. It had been the longest week of her life, she thought.

On Saturday morning she did housework and then went shopping. The shops were packed. Her baskets were heavy enough to contain stones, and her back was aching when she got back to the flat. She was dying for a cup of tea. When she opened the kitchen door, she did not see Steve for a moment, then she stopped dead, staring at him. He was sitting casually at the kitchen table with a cup in his hand.

"I've made some coffee," he said, as if there was nothing more natural in the world than that he should be there waiting for her when she got back with the shopping.

She put her baskets on the table with a sigh of relief before she looked angrily at him. "Will you stop wandering in and out of my flat?"

"I'm going over to see Maggie." He ignored her question without a sign of concern.

"Good." She began to unpack her shopping and heard him move. He poured her a cup of coffee and pushed it across the table.

"What are you doing here?" she asked, and he looked at her through his lashes, a coaxing look in those blue eyes.

"Come with me."

"No."

"Maggie would like to see you. I've talked to her on the phone and she asked me to bring you."

"Oh, did she?" Nicola could imagine. Margaret was always ready to give advice and manage people. It was her life's work, telling other people how to run their lives.

"She's fond of you."

"I'm fond of her," Nicola said, unmoved. "But I am not driving over there with you. I'll visit her some other time, on my own, when you've gone."

The coaxing look went as if it had been switched off. "You obstinate little . . ." He broke off the harsh growl, taking a deep breath.

"I wondered how long the sweet act would last," Nicola said. She never trusted him when he was being reasonable and coaxing. It was always an act. This was the real man, this scowling brute who looked as if he wanted to slap her.

She laid out salad items on the table. Steve glanced at them. "That your lunch?"

"Yes." She added some cheese to the clutter of food. "If you wouldn't mind going, I'd like to eat it, too."

"We could have lunch on the way," he said. "At that little hotel off the road through Essex. Remember? We ate there several times. They have that huge garden and a pond with ducks."

She got down the salad bowl. She remembered all too well. They had walked around the pond one wintry day and fed the ducks ham sandwiches which they had brought but had not eaten. Nicola had a clear picture of the bare willow trees beside the water, the weedy expanse of the pond, the yellow beaks of the ducks as they dived tail-up for the bread.

"They do a fantastic homemade steak pie," Steve said. "And all the vegetables are home-grown, too. I used to think about that place while I was in Africa."

"How charming," Nicola muttered. "I'm glad you were homesick for something." Not her, she gathered. Steve had pined in the steamy African sunshine for homemade steak pie and ducks on a winter pond but he had not yearned for her.

He moved restlessly. "You were part of it," he said huskily. "Part of everything I remembered. When you're on the other side of the world, you have to carry England in your head—green fields and rain and gray London streets." He sounded nostalgic, wry.

"I'm flattered," Nicola said. "It makes a woman feel so appreciated to be added to a list that includes ducks, rain and steak pie." But her smile was slightly shaky and she had to steady her voice. She might not have been a burning memory in his head but she had been there. He hadn't forgotten her altogether. She had suspected he had.

Steve had an impatient cast to his face. He didn't like talking about his feelings. Steve didn't dwell on his softer moments. She sometimes got the impression he would rather not have softer moments at all. His job demanded nerves of steel and a tough independence which was only weakened by emotion.

He stood beside her, watching her, and she could almost hear the little wheels going around in his head. He was trying to work out some way of persuading her to come with him to see Margaret. Nicola looked at the salad. It was a bright spring morning but it was still quite cold and she suddenly did not feel much like eating salad. Steak pie sounded much more tempting.

"The twins and Andrea will be at home," Steve wheedled softly. He knew she enjoyed seeing his sister's children. They were a lively trio, bursting with their mother's vitality, easy to talk to because their extroverted natures made them ready to meet you halfway.

Nicola hated herself. She knew she was weakening. She wanted to go. She wanted to be with him. Looking away, she struggled to force her emotions into line.

The temptation was insidious. It would undermine her, making her strength leach away every time their eyes met. She only really felt strong when she wasn't with him. The masculinity he exuded had a disastrous effect on her.

On the other hand, she told herself hurriedly, going down to see his sister could be a good idea. Steve would find himself wrapped in a warm, happy, family atmosphere which might prove to him that a marriage involved a lot more than the occasional bout of lovemaking in between months of work.

Nicola knew she was just looking for a good reason for doing what she wanted to do. We always have to rationalize our reasons for doing as we like. We snatch at any excuse, however thin, she admitted ruefully to herself.

"Well . . ." she said slowly, and Steve took hold of her elbow, smiling at her.

"Come on," he said, because he knew he had won.

She didn't need to be told he was pleased with himself. His blue eyes made that clear.

Although she let him steer her out of the flat and into the car he had hired, she resented that look. He needn't look so smug. If he thought that driving down to visit his sister was some great triumph, he could think again.

They drove north out of London, along the choked roads, between the rows of little terraced houses back to back, the skyline bristling with television aerials, tiled roofs, chimney pots. This was the shabby hem of London's spreading skirt, a dull sameness about the houses, the shops, the people.

"This is what I go abroad to get away from," Steve confessed, grimacing at it all. "Suburban life in all its deadly boredom."

"You don't have to go abroad to get away from it," she pointed out. "You could live anywhere within reach of London. We could live in the same village as Margaret."

"Heaven forbid," he groaned. "What a prospect."

"That isn't a very kind thing to say about your sister."

"Maggie would drive me to drink inside a month," Steve told her with grim vehemence.

Nicola laughed and he shot her a sideways smile. "And you know it," he added. "She would have you organized in no time. How would you like that?"

Nicola wouldn't, but she didn't bother to admit as much. Steve turned his blue stare back to the road, his mouth crooked.

"And stop trying to get a ring through my nose," he said.

Nicola stiffened, her cheeks reddening. She ignored the little dig but it had hurt.

"Heard from what's-his-name?" Steve asked, after a few moments of silence.

"Martin," she said tersely. "You know very well his name is Martin, so stop calling him what's-his-name."

Steve scowled. "Why should I remember his bloody name? I wish I could forget him."

"Forget away."

"How can I? While I was on the other side of the world you were dating other men."

"Man," Nicola said. "Martin was in the singular."

"So you say."

"It's true," she said angrily. "If it wasn't, I'd tell you. Why should I lie? It's my business how many men I dated, but as it happens, there was only one."

"Well, bully for you," he said with icy dislike.

"Why is it always me who makes confessions? What did you get up to while you were away?" She turned to give him a furious, jealous glare and saw his face relax into amusement.

"Oh, this and that," he said with deliberate, needling mockery.

"Particularly that," she muttered, knowing that satisfied grin. He was pleased to have got that reaction out of her. She shouldn't have betrayed any interest whatever.

"And anyway," she added, remembering, "seeing that we are getting divorced it was my business if I dated someone. I'm not going to apologize to you for it."

"Blast!" he said, putting on a burst of speed which made the tires screech as he took a corner, the hedges on either side of the road masking the view.

They had left the suburban sprawl of London behind them now. They were out in rural Essex, the fields bare and empty, the blue spring sky having that frosty sparkle which gives the light a deceptive brilliance in the cold spring weather. The flat fields of Essex were largely pasture in this corner of the county. Black and white cows grazed under elms and trod heavily over the muddy grass. There were few other cars on these narrow country lanes but Nicola did not enjoy driving fast along them.

"I hope we're not going to argue all the way to Maggie's," Steve muttered.

"Only if you insist," she retorted.

He slowed down, taking a side road, and she asked, "Where are you going now?"

"The hotel, remember? It's somewhere along here."

They found it a few moments later and parked beside a few other vehicles. They had no trouble getting a table. Although the food was good, the hotel was off the beaten track and people did not find it easily.

Steak pie was not on the menu today, but they had a delicious navarin of lamb, a rich stew made with a mixture of spring vegetables, and Steve was content with that.

The hotel dining room was old-fashioned, with heavy plush curtains, paneled walls and a faded dark red carpet. The cutlery was massive silver, worn with use, and the waitress looked as if she had been left over from the Edwardian Age. There was a cathedral hush about the whole place but the excellence of the food more than made up for that.

After they had eaten, Steve insisted on going to look at the duck pond, taking a roll from the table so that he could feed the ducks.

The willows were breaking into tiny bright green knots of leaves. They were alive with birds who flew in and out of the drooping branches. As Steve crumbled his roll and scattered it, the brown ducks fought and squawked, flapping aggressively at each other.

Nicola looked up at the spring sky, shivering in her fur-collared winter coat.

"Cold?" Steve asked.

"A little." It wasn't that, but she was not going to admit it. She felt a peculiar, piercing sadness. That was what had made her shiver.

Steve was laughing as he watched the ducks, his black hair blown across his forehead by the wind. She had one of those unforgettable moments of clarity when a memory is caught like a sharp snapshot in the mind. She knew she would never forget watching Steve today, with the pond and the ducks and the new leaves on the willows behind him.

Her sadness was that of someone recognizing the transitory nature of happiness, the inevitable end of every living organism. Steve was here now, he was alive and amused, but even as she looked at him the moment had ended.

"We'd better get on," he said, turning to her, and she forced a smile and nodded.

He took her arm as she stumbled slightly. "Hey, one glass of wine can't have made you drunk," he said teasingly.

"The path is slippery," she said. "When do you think we'll arrive at Maggie's?"

"I told her any time after lunch."

Margaret would have made elaborate preparations for one of her high teas, then, thought Nicola. Margaret liked to do things properly. The children would have been scrubbed until they shone. The house would be polished from roof to cellar. Margaret's husband, Derek, would be forced into a suit despite his sullen protests. On Saturday afternoons Derek was, given a little luck, free. The patients were given over to the care of another doctor to give Derek some time off. All the doctors in the area organized a rota, which meant they each worked one weekend in four. Derek spent his Saturday afternoons either on the golf course or in his garden, and he hated wearing suits in his spare time.

"Did I show you what I brought her?" Steve asked as they got into the car. He turned and produced a parcel from the back seat.

"Don't unwrap it," Nicola protested. "What is it?"

"An African drum made of deer hide," he said.

Nicola shuddered. "Oh."

Surprised, he asked, "Don't you think she'll like it?"

"She may, I wouldn't," Nicola said. "Every time I looked at it I would think of the poor deer."

Steve grimaced. "I'd forgotten how sentimental you are about animals."

"I'm not sentimental. I just couldn't bear to wear mink coats or have a handbag made out of crocodile."

His blue eyes were amused. "Soft-hearted little idiot," he said.

They drove toward the Suffolk coast through flat green fields punctuated by villages whose narrow streets had been built before the arrival of the motor car. Each one slowed them up as they crawled in a line of traffic through the center of the village. This area of England had once been famous for its wool, and the wealth from the sheep had left a visible legacy in ornate, timbered Elizabethan houses, town halls with high gables and crooked roofs, and great medieval churches left stranded in the fields after the villages around them had died, their spires piercing the blue sky and their high vaulted ceilings echoing with silence.

Margaret lived on the edge of the marshland, the sea within earshot of her house, the trees all bending the way of the wind, their branches crooked and protesting as they creaked.

The children met them at the crossroads, waving their arms and leaping up and down as they spotted the car. Steve slowed and they all climbed into the back.

"Hello, Uncle Steve, Auntie Nicky, what have you brought us?" They had found the packages on the back seat at once and the twins were pinching them inquisitively, exchanging suggestions as to the possible contents.

They were identical boys of seven, thin and small with dark black hair and bright blue eyes and that mixture of toughness and shy tenderness which makes small boys so touching. They hid the tenderness, shoving each other, scrambling to be noticed.

"Sit still," their elder sister commanded, and Peter and Luke made horrible faces behind her back. Andrea was ten, a slim neat girl with the same blue eyes, the same dark hair.

"I'll tell Mummy you asked," she told them. "You know what she told you."

"Those who ask, don't get," Peter repeated. "But this parcel has got Peter on it, so it must be for me." He gave Nicola a crooked little smile and she grinned at him. "How like you the boys are," she told Steve. The twins did not suffer from any inhibitions about presenting their demands, either.

They drove between deep-banked hedges, the air full of the salt scent of the sea, and saw Margaret's house framed between ancient elm trees, the red-tiled roof spotted with yellow lichen. The sea air encouraged the growth, Margaret had once told Nicola.

Margaret appeared through the front door, calm and unruffled in a beige blouse and pearls, a pleated brown skirt, her slim waist drawn in by a leather belt. She looked as casual as though Steve dropped in every day. Kissing him, she said, "Aren't you brown? One look at you and anyone would know you hadn't been in England lately. Did you have a good drive down? How are you, Nicky, you poor girl?"

Steve scowled. "Why is she a poor girl?"

"Married to you," Margaret told him, turning on the twins and asking sharply what they thought they were doing as they began to examine the parcels they had disinterred from the back of the car.

"They can have them," Steve said, taking the parcel containing the drum. "They're labeled."

He needn't have pointed that out. The boys were already tearing them open and giving cries of joy over the intricately carved animals they found inside.

Andrea opened her package to find a set of carved ivory beads which she seemed delighted with and wore at once, kissing Steve as she thanked him.

"Nobody is to play this," Margaret informed the twins with a steely glance as she carried the drum, with which she had been delighted, into the house.

Steve looked down at Nicola. "You see? She liked it."

Nicola was watching the twins fighting as they shoved each other into the house. Steve followed her eyes.

"Brats, aren't they?" he said, and looked at her in

amazement as she gave him a furious glare. "What have I said now?"

"Oh, shut up," she said, walking into the house. She was not going to tell him that she had been thinking how much she envied Margaret the two boys who looked so much like Steve.

Chapter Eight

"Are you serious about this divorce or not?" Margaret asked later as they worked together in the kitchen to prepare the tea. Steve, Derek and the boys had strolled off to take a look at the distant sea from a nearby hill. Andrea had decided to take the opportunity to practice her piano piece. The instrument wasn't exactly in tune; the notes had a dull, flat sound but Andrea made up for that with the great vigor of her performance.

"Yes, I am," Nicola said, skimming plates across the table deftly, but her voice had enough defiance in it to attract Margaret's shrewd little smile.

"Yes?" she questioned, smiling wryly. "You're here with him, though, aren't you? Steve has a maddening habit of getting his own way. He had it in his pram. I'm not sure how he does it. Sheer bloody-minded obstinacy, perhaps."

"He made me come," Nicola said.

"Oh, charming," Margaret grinned.

"Oh, I wanted to see you all," corrected Nicola, laughing. "But I didn't mean to come down with Steve. I'm trying to get it through his head that I'm not living like this anymore. Either he takes me with him or he stays in England, but I'm not putting up with months of separation again."

"What did he say to that?"

"Nothing very pleasant."

"I can imagine," Margaret said. "He's a brute. I remember I warned you about that before you got married." There was always a slight edge to Margaret's voice when she talked about Steve. She was very fond of her brother, but Steve said Margaret had never forgiven him for being born at all. She was a few years his senior, and had enjoyed being an only child. Steve's arrival had put her nose out of joint and she had been resenting him ever since. Their relationship had been a continual struggle for power from the day he was born.

"You stick to your guns," she told Nicola.

Nicola meant to, but she changed the subject. She might find Steve maddening but she wasn't going to let his sister run him down. She had a sneaking suspicion that Margaret was quite enjoying the idea that Steve was not getting things all his own way for once.

The children charged into the kitchen, followed by their father and Steve, and Margaret ordered them all off to wash their hands. They trooped off obediently while Nicola poured the boiling water into the teapot.

The meal was a typical high tea: sandwiches, sliced cold meat, boiled eggs, pickles, several different kinds of cake and a great bowl of fruit salad.

"Did you see any pygmies in Africa?" Peter asked Steve, who grinned at him as he answered. The children were fascinated, staring at their uncle as he talked.

The food disappeared and Margaret presided over them all with regal grace, enjoying having visitors, pleased with Steve's compliments about her food. "No more cake," she told Peter.

"But, Mummy," he groaned, and Nicola watched, moved. There was something magical about sitting here while the windows darkened with the fall of night and the moths flapped at the glass, drawn by the flowering of light inside the room. On the windowsill stood a green glass jar of wild flowers: primroses, violets, early daffodils, the flowers squashed in among tapering sprays of catkins, a mixture of pollen and fresh scent drifting from them.

"We ought to get back," Steve told her.

"Not yet," his sister argued, but Steve insisted that they should leave. It was a two hour drive back to London, he pointed out, and it was nearly seven now.

Everyone crowded out to kiss them good-bye at the car. As they drove away a barn owl flew across the lane, white face peering, the huge span of wings silent on the dark air. Nicola watched it, sighing. She did not feel much like driving back to London or being alone in her silent little flat. She waved to the half-glimpsed faces clustered at the gate and saw the pale hands waving back.

They made good time. It was just before nine when Steve drew up outside the flat. Nicola looked at him with mute hostility.

"Good night."

He frowned, correctly interpreting the chilly note in her voice. "What's wrong now? I thought you enjoyed yourself. You seemed happy."

"I was," she said, and didn't he realize that that was what was wrong? She had been too happy, sitting in that room while the children chattered and ate slices of rich fruitcake, talking of swimming lessons and a motherless lamb at the farm next door, displaying a missing front tooth or giggling over something that had happened at school.

"Then what's up?" he asked.

You're an insensitive, selfish brute, Nicola thought, staying stubbornly silent. That is what is up.

"I thought it was a very good day," he said, tapping his fingers on the steering wheel.

"Oh, did you?" She couldn't help the sarcastic snap of that. It had been more than good—it had been a day lit with poignant beauty for her. The crowded house full of the scent of home cooking, the wild flowers in the jar, the laughter and talk—she had felt it all around her, the distant promise of the sort of life she wanted for them, and that magic had gone now.

"I don't understand you," Steve said, his eyes sliding sideways to study her like some strange specimen under a microscope.

"I know you don't," Nicola told him. "You never have."

"Why can't you tell me what's wrong? Why do you sit there with that blank expression? Do you think I can't see your eyes accusing me? What of, for heaven's sake? What have I done today? I thought you would enjoy visiting Maggie and those awful brats of hers."

Nicola got out of the car and slammed the door, walking very quickly across the pavement. He caught up to her on the doorstep.

"Don't walk out on me when I'm talking," he barked like some army sergeant.

She had her key in her hand and he took it and opened the front door of the flat. Nicola snatched it back. "Good night," she said, starting to shut the door.

He kicked it open again and hurtled past her while she could only fall back, trembling, as she caught sight of his face. Turning, he shoved the door shut and looked down at her, eyes blazing.

"Right—let's have it. What's wrong now?"

"I'm not having another of your violent rows," she told him, stiff as a poker.

He moved so close to her that they were touching. Barely moving his lips he said very softly, "If you don't tell me what is wrong with you, I shall get very violent indeed."

Her eyes fell. "Don't threaten me."

"Don't force me to," he said, caging her in his arms so suddenly that she looked up in alarm.

His blue eyes were smiling now. "You smell of country air," he told her. "Your hair's full of it. Much more attractive than all the scented shampoos in the world."

Her pulses hammered in reaction. "Go away," she said, though. She knew that look in his eyes.

"Throw me out," he invited, grinning.

Helpless, furious, she looked up at him. "You're a brute, do you know that?"

"You keep telling me," he agreed, his lips grazing across her cold pink nose. "Your skin smells of the country too," he said, his mouth making its leisurely way down her cheek. His hands were pressing along her back, holding her tightly.

"Oh, don't," she wailed, far too conscious of the temptation he was presenting.

"Nicky," he muttered, his voice going husky.

She had her hands against his chest. His heart was thudding harshly under her palms.

"Darling, don't send me away again," he whispered, and she listened half to what he said and half to the beating of his heart, the two sounds mingling in her brain.

"I've got to have you," he said. She didn't answer but her whole body shrieked consent although she hoped he could not see it.

He buried his face at the side of her neck, the warmth of his breath on her skin. She thought of the two boys as she had seen them last, their skinny bodies wearing jerseys and short trousers, their wide grins identical as they waved good-bye.

If she told him I want sons like that, I want a home filled with that warmth and happiness, what would he say? Maybe one day, he would promise, because under the urgent pressure of desire he would promise anything. But then he would fly off again and leave her, because Steve's idea of a happy life was not the same as hers and he was not ready to exchange his roaming freedom for the cage of four walls and a wife and children.

"You're driving me mad," he muttered.

What did he think he was doing to her?

"Say something," he ordered, lifting his head to look at her, the blue eyes demanding. "Why do you never say anything?"

"I've said all I have to say," Nicola said. "I'm sick of saying the same thing over and over again."

The telephone rang shrilly. Steve's hands dropped away and Nicola walked to pick the phone up. "Yes?"

"Nicola?" She knew that cautious voice.

"Hello, Martin," she said warmly, and felt Steve stiffen behind her.

"I rang earlier but you were out," Martin said with an undertone of reproach.

"Yes," she said unrevealingly.

"I was going to ask you to have dinner." Martin paused. "Is your husband still around?"

"He isn't staying in the flat," Nicola evaded, and heard Martin give a little sigh of satisfaction.

"Tomorrow, then—will you have dinner tomorrow?"

"I'd love to," Nicola said. "What time tomorrow?"

Steve appeared beside her, his brows together and his blue eyes harsh. He shook his head at her and she ignored him, her expression calm.

"I'll pick you up at seven," Martin said and she told him she would be ready.

As she put the phone down Steve broke out, "I want to see you tomorrow."

"Well, you can't."

"But I'm leaving on Monday," he said, and her heart winced in pain and anger.

Going pale, she repeated, "Leaving? For where?"

"A quick tour of the Middle East," he said.

All she could think was, I've lost. He's going. The words went around and around in her head while she stared at him, her amber eyes wide and fixed, a deep, burning pain behind them.

Steve's brows contracted. "Did you hear what I said?"

"Oh, I heard." Her voice was raw. "What do you want me to say? If you're expecting me to break into floods of tears, too bad. As far as I'm concerned, you can go where you like, when you like. It doesn't matter to me."

His skin ran with angry color. "I see."

"Now, I'm tired. Would you mind going?" She turned away, pretending to give a wide yawn, her hand at her mouth. "Good night. Thank you for the visit to Margaret."

"I'm not going anywhere," he said, catching her elbows and swiveling her around to face him.

"Let go!"

"Oh, no," he said in a deep grim voice. "Not tonight, Nicola; I'm not going anywhere tonight."

Fear concentrated at the back of her throat. She couldn't swallow. Her mouth was dry. She looked up at the darkened face, his bones clenched, the line of his mouth hard and bitter.

"I won't," she muttered.

"We'll see about that." The bitter line twisted in a derisive smile. It was not a smile anyone could enjoy watching. Nicola shivered as she saw it.

There was something pressing at the back of her mind, some vague memory bothering her. The Middle East? she thought. Where did I—and then she remembered, looking at Steve with pain.

"Is Joanne going with you?" The question shot out jealously and she saw his eyes alter, the hardness going and a sudden smile coming into them.

"Yes," he admitted, his mouth mocking.

Nicola winced. She couldn't help it. "I might have known," she said bitterly. "So she got what she was angling for after all, did she?" Joanne had got her foreign posting and Steve all in one. Nicola could imagine how triumphant she must be feeling tonight.

He grinned, watching her. "She worked hard for it—I'd say she deserved to get the job."

"Not to mention you," Nicola snarled. "She worked hard for you, too, didn't she?"

"Careful, sweetheart, you're beginning to sound jealous," he drawled, a gleam in the blue eyes.

"That gives you a kick, does it?" she threw back, her eyes hating him. "You're enjoying this."

His hands shifted to her back, the warmth of them penetrating her shirt and making her nerve ends tingle with awareness. "For tonight let's forget Joanne," he murmured. "Let's forget everything and everyone but us, Nicky."

"Forget? You forget it!" she blazed, pushing him away. "You don't honestly think I'm going to let you touch me when you've just admitted that you're planning to fly off with *her* on Monday, do you?"

"And what about you and what's-his-name?" he asked her coldly, his frown coming back. "You expect me to stand back and watch you dating another man, apparently."

"If you expect me to hang around this flat for months on end without any social life, you're wrong."

"Social life is a new name for it," he grated in a barbed voice. "I know a shorter one."

Her face burned. "For the last time, I have never been to bed with Martin." She looked at him with open hostility. "I can't promise to say the same next time I see you."

The blue eyes iced over. "Don't threaten me, Nicky. I don't like threats."

"Neither do I," she said, nervous under the stare of those cold blue eyes. "I ignore threats."

He moved so suddenly that she was taken by surprise. Swinging her up into his arms he looked down into her paling face. "This is one threat you're not going to ignore," he told her through his teeth.

She opened her mouth to give a yell of fear and anger but he silenced her, his lips clamping over hers and stifling her cry before it could escape. Struggling, she felt him striding across the room. He tossed her on the bed like a doll, the heavy weight of his body pinning her down before she could escape.

Nicola fought in frantic panic, helpless under him, her mouth unable to evade the scorching possession of his kiss. His hands moved slowly over her while she wriggled. She felt her clothes being pulled away and redoubled her efforts to push him off, her face hot, her breathing impeded. She felt she was suffocating and fixed her hands in his thick hair to drag his head away, without success.

"I won't," she groaned against his fierce mouth, but her long fight was weakening her, the writhing of her body lessening. Steve felt her weakening and lifted his head at last. Nicola dragged in air, shuddering, glaring at him.

"You're hurting me," she accused.

"Don't fight me, then," he bit out. "Because you aren't going to stop me tonight, Nicky. You've kept me at arm's length long enough. I should have done this the night I got back but I was too bloody tired. I must have been insane the other day, to go when you told me to get out. I should have taken you then."

"I don't want you," she breathed harshly and he laughed with bitter lack of amusement.

"You're lying and you know it. We both know it."

"No," she said, and then he touched her breast with one long cool finger and her husky, involuntary moan made him laugh again.

"No?"

Nicola closed her eyes, hating herself for that instinctive response. Her lips trembled and the fight drained out of her. What was the point? she thought. He was going. She might never see him again. Did it matter that her suspicions were true? She had always believed that while he was away from her for months at a time he had other women. It might hurt unbearably to know that it was someone like Joanne Hollis but being able to imagine the worst was only one step further down the path to hell. She had been on that path for a long time.

Steve touched his lips to the small hollow at the base of her throat, caressing the fast-beating pulse. "You're mine, that's all that matters." His voice was rough with triumph but the hands touching her were trembling, their seductive movements leaving a track of fire along her body, her skin burning with pleasure everywhere he stroked it.

The sensual trap yawned for her. Nicola tried to make her mind work, tried to escape the coaxing hands, the heated brush of his lips, struggling to remember all her reasons for denying him, but reason fled before the igniting passion Steve had roused in her.

Her arms went around him. She kissed him back, clinging, moving restlessly as desire took over her entire being. Only later, as she moaned with satisfaction, did her drowning mind come up with one sane excuse for giving in to him. Only when she was in his arms did she ever feel alive at all. Wasn't that excuse enough?

She fell asleep in his arms, her head nestled into the hard strength of his shoulder, a hand flung across his muscled chest, aware of the beating of his heart within his ribcage. Steve was already asleep, his long body relaxed against her, the heat of their lovemaking giving way to a tired peace. He had touched his mouth to her hair a moment before he fell asleep, whispering, "I needed that, Nicky. You don't know how I needed you."

He might even mean it. Nicky couldn't guess if he was lying or not, but at this moment she didn't care.

She only knew he was lying close to her, heavy and relaxed, his body warmth reminding her that he was alive, that a moment before they had been one creature briefly.

She woke up during the night to find Steve mumbling and thrashing around beside her, his body twisting on the bed. Was he still having nightmares about what he had seen? She leaned over him, touching his cheek, saying his name gently.

His eyes lifted, gleaming in the darkness, but for a few seconds he did not understand, then he gave a little groan. "Sorry, did I wake you up? Bad dreams again, I'm afraid."

"Would you like me to get you something to drink? Hot milk? Cocoa?"

He smiled wryly. "Just come back here and let me hold you," he whispered, his long arm reaching up to pluck her back into his arms. She settled against him, his cheek against her back, and they fell back to sleep after a short time.

She was alone in the bed when she woke up and stretched, her slim body warm and catlike with sleepy contentment. The curtains were still drawn and sunlight filtered into the room, dancing along the walls like golden water. She curved her arms above her head, a little smile on her lips.

Was Steve making tea? She listened, yawning, but couldn't hear a sound. Maybe he was having a shower, she thought. Slipping out of the bed she put on her dressing gown and went into the kitchen. There was no sign of him. She put on the kettle and as she turned to get the cups out she saw the little note on the table.

It was brief. "Had to rush. Will ring you. Steve."

Nicola's smile vanished. The contented warmth drained out of her, leaving her whole body ice-cold. Gone? Where had he gone? After last night, how could he just walk out on her again, without a word, just a curt little note with no feeling in it? She sank down at the table, her legs trembling under her.

Last night she had weakly abandoned her fight to hold him, allowing Steve to coax her into abject surrender, her pride going down before his with scarcely a struggle.

Now she sat and hated both him and herself. Steve had won. He had achieved the submission he had been determined to wrest from her and she was left with only emptiness. How could I be so weak? she asked herself, her hands clenched.

The phone rang and she leaped up, shaking. Running to answer it, she said nervously, "Hello?"

It wasn't Steve. It was Teddy Wiseman, sounding half asleep, his yawn obscuring his first word. "Sorry," he apologized. "Steve there?"

"No," Nicola said.

"Oh." Teddy sounded embarrassed. "I've been trying to get him at his hotel. They say he wasn't there last night."

"No, he was here," Nicola admitted flatly. "He left some time ago. I don't know where he's gone now."

"Must be on his way to meet Joanne," Teddy said. "Okay, Nicola. Thanks. Sorry to disturb you at this hour on a Sunday."

The phone clicked and he was gone. Nicola looked at the receiver blankly before she replaced it. Steve was with Joanne. Hadn't she suspected it? He had left Nicola in bed and walked out to go to another woman. She slowly walked back into the kitchen and made the tea. If Teddy knew he was meeting Joanne, it must be business, she thought. That made her feel better. A little better—not much. Joanne Hollis was capable of using any weapon at her disposal, even business. Nicola didn't really care why Steve had left her bed to meet Joanne. The fact was that he had, and that his note had given her no glimpse of any warmth or love. It had been a scribbled message, written hastily from the look of the writing. Steve had already forgotten their passion of the night before. His only true passion was his work. That was what separated them, not Joanne Hollis.

Nicola might be his wife, but his job was his mistress, and there was no real doubt as to which he truly loved.

She had a shower and got dressed. The hours passed far too slowly. She waited for the phone to ring but it didn't. By the time Martin arrived, Nicola was in a state of cold misery. She was inclined to tell him she had changed her mind, but why should she sit around the flat waiting for a man who never came and a phone that never rang?

Martin had booked a table at a very expensive restaurant. As they ate, he talked to her about the way he saw the situation. Martin did not rush into such discussions. He laid out his conversation like a railway track. You could see each sentence coming before it arrived.

"I think you owe it to me to be perfectly frank,"

he told her. "You've told me you intend to go through with this divorce, but do you mean it?"

He did not wait for her to answer that. It was, in any case, a rhetorical question. Martin was laying out the facts for her. Only when he had finished would he expect an answer. He had a neat and tidy mind and Nicola looked at him in despair, wondering why she had ever started going out with him.

"I have never believed in romantic love," he said with a faint smile. "Marriages aren't made in heaven. I think you and I could be quite happy together. We get on very well, wouldn't you agree? We're the same sort of people. That's very important in my opinion."

Nicola looked surreptitiously at her watch. Martin talked on and she let the smooth flow of words wash over her head.

He patted her hand, making her start, coming back to him. "So you see, the most essential point is to be very frank with each other."

"Yes," Nicola said. She took a deep breath, "Then, frankly, Martin, we aren't suited at all."

"Oh," he said, looking taken aback.

"You're a very nice man and I like you very much but that isn't enough for marriage and I think we should accept that we aren't suited and just forget about each other."

"I see," he said gravely. "Does this mean you are going back to your husband, after all?"

"No," she said, her smile wavering painfully. "It just means that I should never have started seeing you in the first place and I'm sorry I've wasted so many months of your time. It was my mistake. I am sorry, Martin."

"I think you're wise to stick to your decision to divorce your husband," he told her, a slightly sulky look on his fair-skinned face. "He is a rather nasty type, I'm afraid."

"Yes, he is," Nicola said bitterly. She looked at her watch again, almost relieved to see the inevitable progression of time. "It's getting late," she said. "I'm sorry, Martin, I must go."

They parted as politely as they had met, shaking hands in what she felt to be a rather hilarious fashion. Martin made a little speech about his hopes for her future. "I wish you the best of luck," he told her and she thanked him before she ducked into her flat with a grim sense of relief.

She had known, hadn't she? She had known all along that she felt nothing whatever for Martin. He was a very nice man but he was very dull and she couldn't imagine why she had ever dated him. Martin had felt no more for her than she felt for him. She wondered what he would say if she had told him that she wished for him to experience an encounter with deathless passion? He would smile politely and look amused, no doubt. It would explode like a bomb in his head if he ever fell in love. He didn't believe in the state. Serve him right if he goes crazy over the next girl he sets eyes on, Nicola thought.

There was no sign of Steve. She lay in bed listening for the sound of the phone but it did not ring. It was well into the early hours of the morning before Nicola finally fell asleep and her dreams were troubled. She kept waking up, her eyes hot with misery and lack of sleep.

When the postman came, she flew to the door to see if there was a letter from Steve, but all she received that morning were two bills in brown envelopes. While she got ready for work she kept hoping the phone would ring, but it didn't. She left at the usual time, telling herself that Steve might be at the office when she got there. Her nerves were on edge as she walked into the long, brilliantly lighted room.

There was no sign of Steve as the morning wore on and she finally decided to sink her pride and ring the editorial staff to find out what time his plane left. She sat there thinking up some plausible excuse. It would sear her if everyone knew that Steve had not told her when his plane went, but she could pretend she had forgotten the exact time.

It wasn't necessary. Even as she had made up her mind, Joe came past and smiled at her. She caught up with him as he was making his way into the Morgue.

"When does Steve leave?" She had abandoned all pretense. Joe wouldn't look at her with surprise and curiosity. He wouldn't smile behind his hand.

Joe didn't smile. He hesitated, frowning. "He left last night," he said at last and Nicola took a long, unsteady, bitter breath before she said, "Oh, I see," and walked away feeling like death.

Chapter Nine

It was three weeks later that she discovered she was expecting a baby. Her first reaction was one of stunned disbelief. She had been so bitterly unhappy over Steve's sudden departure that it hadn't even occurred to her that she might have become pregnant. Once she had realized it, though, a fierce happiness filled her for a day or two. She wanted Steve's baby. She had wanted it for a long time. For months she had looked into prams and felt envious. Knowing that new life was growing inside her gave her a strange, tremulous pleasure.

Only later did she realize the irony of it. It was one of fate's little jokes. But Nicola was not laughing. She was facing the practical problems the baby would bring and she was feeling disturbed.

She had to talk to someone, but she refused to make a confidante of anyone in the office. That weekend she caught the train to Suffolk to see Margaret.

The house was sunny and full of the scent of bluebells. The children had picked them in a nearby wood, cramming the pale green stalks together into a vase, the deep blue of the flowers trembling as a spring wind blew through the open window.

Margaret had been baking bread. The golden brown loaves stood on a baking tray on the table in the kitchen. Margaret made coffee while Nicola looked out at the children. They were playing in the garden, their shouted words floating back to the house. Derek was out on his rounds through the local villages. A black spaniel slept under the table, his nose on his paws. Nicola sighed.

"What's wrong?" Margaret asked, pushing a cup of coffee across the table. "Have a doughnut?" They were hot, their surfaces coated with sugar. Nicola looked at them, shuddering.

"No, thank you. I'm not hungry."

"You look pale," Margaret decided, eyeing her. "I'm glad to see you, but why are you here? Something's up, I suppose? Steve? He hasn't had an accident again, has he?"

"No," Nicola said, pausing. "I have."

Margaret stared. "You've had an accident?" Her eyes ran over Nicola in surprise. "What sort of accident? What are you talking about?"

"I'm going to have a baby." Nicola had been rehearsing it all the way down in the train but she felt self-conscious and silly as she said it, all the same.

Margaret gave a whoop of amazement and pleasure. "No! You're not? That's . . ." She broke off, meeting Nicola's strained amber eyes. "That's complicated things," she finished more soberly.

"Hasn't it though?" Nicola tried to laugh but didn't quite make it.

"What are you going to do?" Margaret was frowning now, the excited look no longer in her face.

"I don't know," Nicola confessed.

"Are you still going on with the divorce? You can't, Nicky. You can't divorce him when you're expecting his baby."

"Can't I?" Nicola nursed her coffee cup in both hands, watching the way the bluebells swayed on the windowsill, their heavy perfume drifting to her nostrils.

"Oh, Nicky," Margaret said, her tone torn between reproach and sympathy.

"What will happen if I tell him? He'll be cock-a-hoop. He'll think he's won. I'll have to stay at home to look after the baby and Steve will carry on just the way he always has, flying around the world, living like a bachelor except when he's in London when he'll expect me to offer him home comforts until he's ready to clear off again."

Margaret listened to the hurried, impassioned words, frowning. She sorted out the only thing that made sense to her. "Don't you want to have the baby?"

Nicola looked at her with pain. "Of course I do. I want it badly. But that doesn't alter anything, does it?"

With maddening common sense, Margaret shrugged. "I'd say it did. The baby is a fact. You're going to need Steve's help whether you divorce him or not. You can't manage to bring up a baby on your own; don't be silly."

Nicola hadn't told her about Joanne. She wasn't going to, either. Margaret would be deeply shocked. She had old-fashioned ideas about marriage, ideas Nicola shared, and although Margaret might call Steve a callous brute, she was fond of her brother. Nicola wasn't about to destroy Margaret's respect for Steve.

"I'll manage somehow," she said stubbornly.

Margaret spent the rest of the time trying to persuade her to change her mind about the divorce. "I'm sure that when Steve knows, he'll stay in England," she said.

Nicola knew it would make no difference. Steve wasn't going to let a little thing like a baby stop him from leading the sort of life he enjoyed, and Nicola wasn't going to try to use the baby as a weapon against him. If Steve wasn't prepared to stay with her for her own sake, she wasn't going to blackmail him. Her pride wouldn't let her.

She spent the whole weekend in Suffolk. On Sunday she and the twins walked through the fields with fitful sunshine illuminating the stormy horizon. When they got back, Derek had mowed the lawn and the garden had that pungent odor of newly cut grass. Derek had gone to sleep in a deck chair and the twins tiptoed up to drop grass cuttings onto his face. Nicola went in to help their mother, laughing.

She did not want to go back to London. Her flat was so empty, as empty as her life, and although she was laughing, her eyes were weary. Margaret looked at her with sudden anxiety.

"You will look after yourself, won't you Nicky? I don't like the idea of you alone in London now."

Nicola hurriedly dragged a smile across her face. "I'll be fine," she lied with vehemence.

Steve was already sending back stories from the Middle East, but Nicola did not read them. Whenever her eye was caught by his byline she skipped past hurriedly, frowning. She could only manage not to think about him if she avoided him deliberately.

It was quite easy while she was at work. She could keep busy, her mind occupied by other things. But when she got home to the empty flat, the dead weight of that silence fell on her and her heart ached with misery.

People carefully did not mention either Steve or Joanne, but Nicola couldn't help noticing the gaps in their conversations. If there were reporters talking in the canteen and Steve's name came up, there would be a hurried change of subject if any of them noticed Nicola at a nearby table.

Everyone knew, of course. How could they help knowing? Steve and Joanne were out there together and, knowing Joanne, there could be little doubt as to what was going on between them.

Nicola heard next to nothing from Steve. That didn't surprise her. He hated writing letters; he always had. She got a few postcards with snappy little messages on them. She tore them up.

One afternoon as she left the building a car drew up beside her and she looked around to recognize Joe, grinning from ear to ear. "Like a lift home?"

Nicola was tired. She felt tired quite often these

days. Her doctor had given her some iron tablets and scolded her because he thought she wasn't eating enough. She had lost more weight when she should have begun to put some on, he said.

Joe watched her settle herself in the passenger seat, doing up her seat belt. "It's very kind of you," she told him, smiling. She hadn't seen much of him lately. He had been up in Scotland working on a big trial which had just ended.

"I've got a space in the car park at last," Joe said cheerfully. "I've only been waiting for three years." Space was very limited in the underground car park beneath the office block and a parking pass was highly coveted.

She congratulated him. "How did you pull that off?"

"I think it's a mistake," Joe said, laughing. "But I'm not arguing. It means I can bring my car into town and I'm sick of public transport."

Summer had come to the city. The girls wore light summery dresses and the floods of tourists had begun to swarm through the streets. It had been hot all day and Nicola pushed her hair back from her perspiring forehead.

"This weather is tiring," she said.

"You get paler every time I see you," Joe murmured, looking at her sideways. He frowned. "Are you okay, Nicola?"

She felt as if she was being dragged away, her body weak and slack, her head strangely buzzing. Forcing a little smile she told him she felt fine.

He wasn't convinced, watching her from time to

time as he drove, and she struggled to make polite conversation. I am not going to faint, she told herself firmly.

Joe pulled up outside her flat and she thanked him before she got out of the car, stumbling a little as the bronze gong of the sun beat down on her head. Joe got out and caught up with her, putting an arm around her.

"Are you ill?"

She lifted her aching head wearily. "No, of course not, it's this heat." The heat, the noise of the city, the long hours spent in the overcrowded office—they had all contributed to her lack of energy.

Joe took her key and opened the flat door. Nicola walked inside rather unsteadily, leaned on the wall with one hand, her head bent to recover her balance. The hallway was going around like a washing machine. She felt dizzy, sick.

Leaving the door open Joe hurried to put an arm around her again. "You *are* ill," he said anxiously, his hand over her dark head.

Nicola felt him turn her. She swayed forward and let her head droop onto his chest. Her legs seemed to be sliding out from under her. She clung to Joe to keep herself upright.

Sudden panic poured through her. Am I going to lose my baby? The very idea of that made her realize how much she wanted it, how badly she would feel if she lost it now. Whatever the problems, she wanted to have Steve's baby. It would kill her if she lost it.

"I'll get a doctor," Joe told her, stroking her hair.

He guided her through the flat and made her lie down on her bed. The room was still going around.

She kept her eyes shut, shivering. She could hear Joe talking on the phone, then he came into the room and looked at her. "Just lie still," he whispered with touching anxiety. "The doctor will be here soon."

Nicola wanted to sit up and assure him that she was fine, just a bit tired; she muttered incoherently, her voice just barely audible, and Joe bent over her to push her back against the pillow. "You stay where you are," he said. "You're as white as a ghost."

"The heat," Nicola whispered.

"Yes," said Joe, unconvinced.

It was easier to keep her eyes shut. The room stayed still and she didn't have to be afraid she was going to be sick. Joe had gone away, she thought. She couldn't hear him breathing and that meant she could relax. She just lay there, waves of tiredness breaking over her head.

"Now, then, what's all this?" The new voice broke in on her and she forced her eyes open to see her own doctor bending over her.

"Hello," he said cheerfully. "How do you feel now?"

Nicola's mouth felt numb and cold. "The baby," she asked. "Am I going to lose the baby?"

"Why should you think that?" He was a kind man, in his late fifties, very sensible and calm. He asked her questions and she answered them, but she kept sliding away into that dull silence which waited for her every time she shut her eyes.

"A few days in bed for you," the doctor told her.

She looked at him again, blinking as she tried to focus her eyes on him. "Is the baby all right?"

"Everything seems to be fine," he assured her.

"But you've been a very silly girl, haven't you? Not been eating, have you? Your face is gaunt, all bones. What did I tell you? You can't skip meals or the baby will suffer. I want you to stay in bed and eat three sensible meals a day, plenty of milk and fresh vegetables and protein. I'll give you a diet sheet, but for the moment just get some rest."

Nicola was already far away before he had finished talking. She didn't hear him leave. The silence beat around her and she gave in to it with relief.

It was dark in the room when she opened her eyes again. She cautiously sat up. Her head wasn't going around anymore but she felt sick. It was a different sickness now. She was sick with hunger.

She slowly slid out of the bed and began to get undressed. She had slept in her clothes and they were horribly creased. When she had put on a nightie and dressing gown, she walked unsteadily to the door. It opened as she got to it, and with a gasp of amazement she looked at Joe.

"Hey, what are you doing out of bed?' he asked.

"What are you doing here?" she asked in her turn. She had imagined he had gone. She thought he had left with the doctor, if not before.

"Someone had to stay with you." Joe looked sheepish. "I couldn't leave you alone in that state."

"Oh, you are kind," Nicola said, giving him a quavering little smile. "Thank you, Joe, but there's no need to stay now. I'm fine again."

"It's no problem," he said. "Can I get you anything? A drink? Something to eat?"

She tried to persuade him to go but Joe was being

obstinate, and in the end she had to accept that he was staying.

She made her way to the bathroom, pausing several times as she felt giddy, but when she had washed and brushed her hair she felt much better. She got back into bed ten minutes later and Joe brought her some scrambled eggs and toast. He sat on the end of the bed to watch her eat, as though suspecting she wouldn't eat at all if she wasn't under surveillance.

She managed to eat it all, smiling at him as he took the tray. "That was very nice. Thank you."

"You look a little better, less like a ghost. You really had me scared, you know." He smiled at her as she lay down against the pillows. "There wasn't a scrap of color in your face." She could tell from his solicitous manner that the doctor had told him about the baby. Joe was walking about on tiptoes, almost like an expectant father. He fussed over her covers, tucking her in again, and Nicola smiled up at him.

"You are a darling, Joe."

A harsh voice sounded from the doorway as she finished speaking. "What's going on here?"

Joe straightened and spun around, his face flushing a dark red. Nicola sat up, the covers falling back from her bare shoulders, her pallor only increasing as she looked across the room and saw Steve. His face was pale, too, the lines of it harsh, his blue eyes glittering in molten anger.

"Well?" he demanded when neither of them spoke. His stare flicked to Joe, his lip curling back from his teeth. "What are you doing in my wife's bedroom?" He looked at his wristwatch. "It's two o'clock in the bloody morning—what's going on?"

"Don't shout at Joe," Nicola said coldly. How could he have the nerve to behave like a jealous husband after all he had done? He was a hypocrite. She looked at him with scathing distaste and Steve stared back at her, the flare of a barbaric fury in his blue eyes.

"Shout at him?" he repeated. "I'll break his neck."

Joe looked nervous and shuffled back a little. "I know what it must look like, Steve," he began in a worried voice, and Steve's eyes spat bitter hostility at him.

"But it isn't like that," Joe added hurriedly. He was a mild man with no taste for violence and he could see in Steve's eyes that any minute violence was what was going to happen. Steve was standing in rigid menace, his long body taut with a desire to break things, principally Joe's neck.

"Don't tell him anything, Joe," Nicola interrupted coolly. "It isn't any of his business."

"The devil it isn't," Steve shouted hoarsely, his stabbing blue eyes turning toward her.

"Don't you come into my flat shouting and swearing at this hour of the night," Nicola said. "Joe is here at my invitation. You aren't."

That seemed to leave him speechless. He breathed audibly, his jaw clenched, looking at her as though he did not know her. After a moment he ground out, "How could you, Nicky? How could you let anyone else touch you?"

"Why shouldn't I? You have no right to criticize me. If you can, I can, so go back to Joanne Hollis and don't come anywhere near me again. I hate the very sight of you."

Joe had listened to their exchange with an embarrassed, worried face. Even his ears looked red. Now he moved toward Steve, saying nervously, "Don't take any notice of her, she isn't herself. I'll explain."

"I don't need any explanations," Steve said murderously, his sinewy hands clenching. "Save your breath. You're going to need it when I choke you to death."

"She's having a baby," Joe croaked, stepping back quickly, fear in his eyes.

For a few seconds Steve looked at him, his blue eyes narrowing, then he abruptly moved across the room to the bed. Nicola shrank back in it, looking up at him with icy defiance.

"Is that true?"

She didn't answer. She had nothing to say to him. Joe moved away to a safe distance, and after a moment said, "It is true, Steve. She fainted earlier and I got her doctor. He told me."

"It's mine," Steve said, only the faintest question in his voice, as though he knew already.

Nicola looked away, her mouth mutinous.

"She hasn't been eating," Joe said. "The doctor is worried about it. She's losing weight all the time."

"Get out, Joe," Steve said, without moving his eyes from her.

"But," Joe began and Steve repeated the curt order.

"Get out—and get out now."

"Don't talk to him like that," Nicola said. "Joe, don't go. He can't give orders in my home."

"Unless you want his head twisted off his neck, I'd advise you to be quiet," Steve said softly.

Joe hesitated, looking at her. "If you want me to stay . . ."

Steve swung, tense and dangerous, and Nicola said hurriedly, "You'd better go, Joe. Thank you for being so kind. I'm very grateful."

Joe nodded, looking back at her with anxious eyes, then he went out, closing the door.

Steve bent toward her, talking through tightly closed lips, his voice very low and rough. "You stupid little fool."

"I must be a fool to have married you."

"I ought to wring your neck," he said, then he sat down on the bed and stared at her, his eye traveling from her ruffled hair down her pale shoulders, the half-revealed breasts in the candy pink nightie, the pallor of her hands as she grabbed at the covers to haul them up against herself.

"You look terrible," Steve muttered. "What have you been doing to yourself?"

"What have *I* been doing to myself?" She gasped that in sheer incredulity.

"You're too thin and you look ill."

"And none of that would be your fault, would it?" she asked with bitter sarcasm.

His blue eyes closed and he gave a thick deep sigh. "I'm sorry," he muttered.

It made her even angrier to hear him say that. "I

don't want you anywhere near me," she told him with hatred.

"After I've flown halfway across the world to get to you?" Steve murmured wryly, opening his eyes and looking at her with a faint, coaxing smile.

"What are you doing in London again so soon? Tired of Joanne, Steve? Or did she ditch you and go off with someone else?" Her voice was full of barbed cynicism and he frowned.

"I hate to hear you talking like that. There was never anything between me and Joanne."

She laughed disbelievingly.

"There wasn't," he insisted. "Oh, Joanne was stalking me, all right, but her motive wasn't what you thought. She wanted to use me to get herself a job on foreign. She knew that if I moved back to London, there would be a vacancy. She wanted to persuade me to take the Deputy's job and leave a place that she could fill."

Nicola had already worked out a lot of that, but she knew Joanne fancied him. She had seen Joanne doing it, all too obviously, giving him come-hither smiles and flirtatious little glances.

"But you wanted her," she said thickly, biting her inner lip.

"I've never wanted Joanne," he muttered. "She's not my type at all." He looked at her through lowered black lashes, his face taut. "*You're* my type, except when you're shouting. I like my ladies to be soft and warm and feminine, not tough go-getting creatures like Joanne Hollis."

Nicola stared at him, wondering how much of that

to believe. "You've been with her for weeks," she accused.

"Taking her on a quick tour of her new district," Steve told her.

"What?" Nicola sat up, her eyes fixed on him.

"Joanne was taking over the job, not me," he said. "I was just there to give her some training, teach her some of the tricks of the job. I've left her nicely settled in a flat in Cairo."

"You aren't going back there?" Joanne was a matter of supreme indifference to Nicola now.

He shook his head, his blue eyes taking on a glint. "I've got a new base."

Her face froze. "Oh?" Not Africa again, she thought dully. Where was he flying off to now?

"Aren't you interested?" He leaned back, his hands propping him up and his lean body languidly at ease as he watched her. "Don't you want to know about my new job?"

Her heart leaped into her mouth. "You're taking the London job?" Hope made her voice shake but it went as he shook his head, smiling. She felt her skin quiver with icy nerves. "Where, then?" What did it matter, though? He wasn't going to be here with her. She was going to have her baby alone while Steve diced with death in some distant part of the world.

"Washington," he said.

Nicola was too stunned to speak, her eyes fixed on him almost pleadingly. "Washington?"

"The plum job," he said, grinning. "I've been angling for it for years but Don Sutcliffe was a fixture out there. He didn't want to come home and he was too good for the paper to move him if he wanted to stay. But his wife's parents are in their seventies and Linda has been nagging Don to bring her home so that she can visit them more often. Don finally caved in and asked for a transfer back to London."

Nicola could scarcely breathe.

Steve looked at her with sardonic amusement. "Women are a pain in the neck," he said, smiling. "They always get their own way."

"Do they?" Nicola's voice was very small and husky.

He leaned forward to run his fingers down the pale curve of her cheek. "Always," he said. "Do you think you'll enjoy living in Washington?"

"Yes," she said, before he could change his mind. "When do we go? I can be ready tomorrow."

He grinned, his mouth crooked. "No rush. Don doesn't come home until next month. That gives us time to sell this place or put it on the market anyway, and pack up the things you want to take over to the States."

Nicola was weak with relief and happiness, but under that glow of joy she still felt angry with him. "Why didn't you tell me this was in the wind? Why did you go off without a word last time? How could you do that to me?"

Steve looked at her for a moment without saying anything, then he sighed. "I hadn't made up my mind. I had a lot of thinking to do. You were right when you said I hadn't wanted to change my life-style after we were married. I liked the way I lived and I didn't want to alter anything. You made me see I couldn't go on doing things the way I'd always done them."

"Why couldn't you tell me what you were thinking?"

"I needed to think away from you." He looked at her with a frown. "Nicky, I've been a selfish brute. You were right. When I got caught in that massacre and thought I wasn't coming out of it alive, I realized how much more you meant to me than I'd ever admitted to myself. I realized how much I needed you, how much I loved you."

Her heart began to thud with violent happiness. She put a hand out toward him and he moved closer, encircling her with his arm, pushing her head down onto his shoulder, his hand stroking her hair.

"You're everything I've ever wanted in a woman," he whispered, brushing his lips across the stray strands of ruffled hair. "The minute I saw you I knew you were the woman for me. The trouble was, I didn't want to give up my job. I tried to have you and my job as well, and it didn't work, did it?"

"No, it didn't," she said huskily, but her voice was light because she had won, after all. She had suffered in the process but the final victory was hers and she could forgive him anything.

"I know I kept arguing with you last time I was here, but underneath I was thinking, and beginning to realize that I had to accept that I had to settle down. I was angry with you, I suppose. I love you like mad, my darling, but I wanted to have my cake and eat it too, as you rightly said. Even while I was quarreling with you I was admitting to myself that it was all up with me. I knew I'd have to find a way for us to be together."

A sigh wrenched her. "For weeks I've been thinking you were with Joanne. It seemed the obvious conclusion." She moved away to look at him with angry accusation. "You must have known that that was what I was going to think. You deliberately let me suffer like that."

He grimaced, a wry apology in his blue eyes. "I'm sorry, darling. I was a bit resentful, I guess. All those rows we had when I was here last—I'd flown home with one thought in my mind, desperate to hold you in my arms again. Almost getting killed in Africa made me face the way I needed you. I'd have told you if you'd let me, but instead, from the minute you set eyes on me, you were spitting at me like a little cat and it made me mad."

"So you tried to make me jealous by flirting with Joanne," she said dryly.

Wicked amusement glinted in his eyes. "Tried? I succeeded, didn't I?"

"It wasn't funny," Nicola retorted, frowning at him.

"Don't glare," he said softly. "I told you she doesn't turn me on. The only person in the world Joanne cares about is herself. I'm not into ambitious ladies with an eye to the main chance. Not many men are."

"Joanne does all right," Nicola muttered, remembering watching the other woman turning her come-hither smiles on him and getting an amused response.

He looked sharply at her; his smile vanished.

"You believe me, don't you? Nicola, since the day I met you there's never been another woman."

"Never?" she probed, watching him closely. Ever since their marriage she had been troubled by doubts on that subject.

His eyes met hers frankly, directly. "I swear to you," he said. "I've never even looked at anyone else. I know I didn't write to you often—I'm not a letter-writer. But you were never out of my thoughts. I missed you all the time, especially lately. I'd have had you with me if it hadn't been so dangerous. You're so small and soft." He cupped her face in his hands, looking at her passionately. "I was scared stiff something might happen to you."

"Do you think I wasn't scared stiff? Do you think I didn't stay awake at night wondering if you were lying dead somewhere?" Nicola's voice shook.

He sighed wryly. "I know. I should have realized what it was doing to you but I was blind. I kept telling myself that you'd known what sort of life I led when we married so you must be able to cope with it. I couldn't believe you meant it when you said you were going to divorce me. I knew you still loved me. I thought you were just making idle threats. I thought that next time I came back we'd have a serious talk about it."

"You were behaving selfishly, you mean," she informed him with impatience.

"Yes," he said almost humbly. "I'm sorry, Nicky."

"So I should think." She looked at him through her lashes and he watched her, his strong face anxious.

"Don't go on being angry, darling," he coaxed. "Forgive me."

Her mouth curved in a teasing little smile. "I'll consider it. You are glad about the baby, aren't you? You haven't said a thing about that yet."

"I haven't had time to think about it," he said slowly. "I suppose I am. The baby makes the last link in the chain, doesn't it? I'm bound hand and foot. There's no escape for me anymore." He smiled at her, though, his eyes wry.

Nicola looked at his strong-boned, bronzed face with passionate intensity. "Do you still want to escape, Steve?" Wasn't that what it had all been about? He had married her because he fell in love with her but he had still wanted to escape. Their real struggle had begun only after their marriage. Steve had got married without intending to change his life at all. Was he, even now, really ready to accept that he was no longer a free man?

"That's what I had to decide," he told her. "That's what I went away to think about. And I had to face the fact that I could only be free if I left you—and I knew I would never be able to do that. I would kill anyone else who touched you. You belong to me." He looked at her, smiling. "And logic made me admit that, in that case, I belonged to you and I was no longer free anyway. I just hadn't come around to admitting it. It was all quite simple in the end."

"I wish I'd known this was going on inside your head," Nicola sighed. "The last weeks haven't been easy for me." She was understating with deliberate intention. She wasn't going to admit to him that she had almost gone out of her mind with pain.

"I'll make it up to you," he promised huskily, putting his lips against her bare shoulder, then his head came up and his mouth sought hers, kissing her fiercely, possessively, with a desire which made her tremble. "My love," he muttered. "When I came in here tonight and saw you in bed and Joe there—I thought I'd go crazy. I was so jealous I could hardly see straight."

"Poor Joe, you scared him silly."

"Serves him right," Steve said.

"He was being very kind to me," she protested, opening her eyes wide.

"He can be kind to someone else," Steve muttered. "He isn't offering any more kindness to my wife."

"You can't suspect poor Joe . . .?"

"Oh, can't I?" Steve looked at her dryly. "Poor Joe has been carrying a torch for you for months."

Nicola blushed and he gave her a probing stare. "Don't tell me you hadn't noticed? You're just the sort of girl Joe fancies—he must have thought it was his birthday, being here alone with you while you were in bed."

"That's very unfair," she said. "Joe behaved very well."

Steve grinned at her. "If you can be jealous, so can I. For one sinking moment I thought . . ." He broke off, his face hardening again. "It occurred to me that you might have started an affair with Joe out of revenge. You threatened to, remember? When I saw you together, that was the first thought in my head and I was ready to commit murder."

"I didn't mean it," Nicola admitted, linking her arms around his neck. "I love you too much."

"Not too much," Steve said thickly. "Never too much, my darling. I need every bit of love you've got." He kissed her throat, his lips heated. "And I need it now. If you weren't so ill, I'd do something about getting it, too, but it must wait."

"I'll be much better tomorrow," she promised, smiling.

"Tomorrow, then," he whispered, as he began to kiss her mouth. Only a few hours ago, Nicola thought, she had been in the depths of a grim and bitter misery but suddenly the world had turned on a new axis and her future was bright with promise. She had been so afraid that all she would have were those brief, burning memories. Instead she had a crowded procession of tomorrows stretching in front of her, each of them crammed to the brim with happiness.